TWISTED TALES: A RUSSIAN FAIRY TALE COLLECTION

The Three Horsemen of the Black Forest
Fire of the Four Seasons

Scarlet Hyacinth

MENAGE AMOUR
MANLOVE

Siren Publishing, Inc.
www.SirenPublishing.com

A SIREN PUBLISHING BOOK
IMPRINT: Ménage Amour ManLove

TWISTED TALES: A RUSSIAN FAIRY TALE COLLECTION
The Three Horsemen of the Black Forest
Fire of the Four Seasons
Copyright © 2011 by Scarlet Hyacinth

ISBN-10: 1-61034-803-6
ISBN-13: 978-1-61034-803-4

First Printing: August 2011

Cover design by Jinger Heaston
All cover art and logo copyright © 2011 by Siren Publishing, Inc.

Printed in the U.S.A.

PUBLISHER
Siren Publishing, Inc.
www.SirenPublishing.com

DEDICATIONS

The Three Horsemen of the Black Forest

For everyone who's ever read a fairytale and wanted the prince to end up with his best friend, not the princess.

With thanks to Rachel, Kyo, Alice, and my Puy for their support and suggestions.

Fire of the Four Seasons

For everyone who read my first ménage story ever, *The Three Horsemen of the Black Forest*. May your life always be a beautiful fairytale, preferably involving lots of lovin' and hot men ☺

Siren Publishing

Ménage Amour

The
Three Horsemen
of the
Black Forest

Scarlet Hyacinth

For some reason, his dark gaze made Larissa feel petty and insignificant. Larissa nodded quietly. Smiling in obvious relief, Deni took a deep breath and started to explain once more. "Your son is meant for great things. His future is bound to ours and his happiness to our freedom."

Larissa couldn't really understand what Deni meant by that cryptic statement. Before she could voice her questions, Sonta took a step forward and took hold of her palm. His hand felt hot, almost scorching to the touch. Even so, strangely enough, the heat didn't burn her. In fact, it comforted her. Sonta squeezed her hand, allowing the warmth to seep through her body.

"For that to happen, Vassili will need help," Sonta pointed out. "He will encounter things in life, enemies difficult to defeat."

Noci approached once more, his tone turning calmer, friendlier. "Through you, we will gift Vassili with an important, very valuable gift." Noci leaned toward the wooden chest where Dimitri kept his carvings and retrieved a toy soldier. Dimitri had carved it just a few days ago for their unborn son. "The gift we entrust to you now must be kept a secret at all costs."

Deni nodded, placing his palm over the toy soldier in Noci's hand. "You must not tell anyone about our presence here."

Sonta finally released Larissa from his grip and added covered Deni's hand with his own. "Not even Dimitri, not even Vassili himself."

A light started to shine from the palms of the three mysterious men. Black, white, and red surrounded the little toy soldier. For a second, Larissa thought it would be destroyed by the onslaught of power. It didn't happen. When the light died, Deni and Sonta lifted their hands off the toy, and Noci handed it to Larissa.

Larissa glanced at it skeptically. It didn't look any different. "This is the gift for Vassili?"

Before the three men could answer, a different voice replied. "Yes, beautiful Larissa. I am the gift for your son."

Larissa gasped as the wooden soldier spoke, dropping it to the floor. Noci lifted it back up and Deni chuckled at the little toy's slightly put-out expression. It seemed incredible that a toy soldier could even have an expression, but there it was.

"We gave our little friend here life, wisdom, kindness, and strength," Noci explained. "He will be a valuable aid for your Vassili."

The wooden soldier nodded. "Whenever he gets into trouble, he'll just have to feed me and I will help him with his predicament."

Sonta took a step forward and gave Larissa a serious look. "Gift the soldier to Vassili when he comes of age. The toy will guide your son on the path he needs to take."

Noci placed the toy back in Larissa's hand. It once again became just a wooden, lifeless soldier. "Do not worry, Larissa. We mean well. You can feel it in your heart."

Larissa took another glance at the soldier. She did feel apprehensive about the magic she'd seen them do. However, Noci was right. In her heart, she somehow knew these men would be linked to Vassili's future. "All right," she whispered with a smile. "I will give it to him."

Noci smiled back, for the first time actually appearing to be satisfied. Taking a step back, he gripped Deni's hand and then Sonta's. Before Larissa's very eyes, the three mysterious men disappeared.

Chapter 1

Vassili knelt by the bed, his eyes on the fragile, pale figure resting before him. His dear, sweet mother. He still couldn't believe that she had fallen so ill. The strong, healthy, and happy woman who told him stories when he went to bed somehow turned into a shadow of her former self. She could no longer tuck him in or sing to him. In fact, she could barely speak now.

Vassili struggled to be strong and not burst into tears as he caressed his mother's face. She would soon be on her feet once more. The doctor had given them medicine and it would make her feel better.

Suddenly, Larissa cracked her eyes open, blinking a bit as if to focus her vision. She smiled at Vassili, urging him closer. "My dear son," she began softly, "I fought this thing that consumed me for so long, but I cannot fight it any longer. God is calling for me to join him."

Tears started flowing on Vassili's cheeks, for he knew that his mother was finally giving up the fight. Even so, he tried to protest Larissa's words. "No, Mama, I will call Papa. We will get the doctor."

Larissa coughed and held on to Vassili's hand. "No, my dear Vassili, stay here with me. I have something for you."

With that, Larissa retrieved one of Vassili's carved toy soldiers from under the blanket. Vassili saw his mother had sewn the soldier pretty blue clothes that matched his own eyes, adorning them with shining buttons. "Take it, *cyn*. If you ever get into trouble, prepare some food and feed it to the soldier and he will help you."

Dimitri walked in, his face paling visibly when he saw the tears on Vassili's cheeks and Larissa's glassy eyes. "No! No, Larissa, you cannot give up."

The sick woman gave her husband a small smile. "I am so sorry for leaving you, *lubov moya*. The illness has consumed me, and I cannot hold on any longer."

Dimitri's hands trembled as he opened a drawer and retrieved a candle. Almost automatically, he lit it and placed it on the nightstand. He turned toward his son and gave him a lost look. "Vassili, go to the village. Find the priest."

"No." Larissa clutched Dimitri's hand and beckoned Vassili back. "Too late now. Just stay here, keep me company. God loves me either way." She took a deep breath, her eyes turning a bit dazed as she struggled to speak. "And when I'm gone, bury me in the grove, so I can always be here."

His eyes swimming with tears, Dimitri pressed his mouth to his wife's in a desperate kiss. She died, giving her last breath into her kiss with her beloved Dimitri.

Vassili just stared in disbelief as his father collapsed on top of his mother's still body. It couldn't be. His mother couldn't be dead. She promised she would always be by his side.

He didn't know how long he stayed like that, clutching the wooden soldier in his hand. Eventually, he became aware of his father getting up and caressing his mother's face. His father's hand passed over Larissa's face, closing her eyes. Without a word, he exited the room. Vassili took one look at his mother's body and ran out, suddenly feeling too afraid to even see Larissa. He watched as his father rummaged through some coffers and revealed a beautiful set of clothing and a large, white sheet.

Dimitri then turned to look at Vassili. "Go to the church and get the priest. We need to…With this heat, we need to bury her as soon as possible." He swallowed, looking away, clutching the material of the clothes so tight his knuckles went white. "And let her family know."

Vassili opened his mouth to say something, anything, but he couldn't speak. In the end, he just ran out, realizing that he was much better off doing this task than seeing his mother be prepared for burial.

Vassili didn't know how he managed to fulfill the task his father gave him. At some point, everything became a blur. His body seemed to be working automatically, while his mind retreated someplace remote. He distantly acknowledged the well-wishes and offers for help. When he finally returned to their cottage, he blankly watched relatives and friends arrive, giving Larissa her last farewell. The next morning, they dug her a grave in the grove behind the house, according to her wishes. It would be marked by a cross carved by Vassili's father, to forever keep her kindness and beauty in their memory.

After all was said and done, Dimitri wept for weeks and weeks after his lost wife. Vassili could hear him every night, going to Larissa's grave, calling out her name into the darkness. Even in the mornings, Dimitri would wonder around, an absent expression on his face, completely ignoring Vassili. For a while, Vassili lost himself in his own grief and he hoped that he would, eventually, manage to get his father back. However, when Dimitri finally stopped weeping, Vassili saw that his father had changed. He was no longer the happy woodcarver who made him toy soldiers. He was now a cold man, dead inside, his spirit crushed by the loss of his beloved wife. Vassili received no more smiles and his childhood became as chilly and barren as his mother's grave.

A few years passed in the now lonely cottage. As much as Vassili tried to find a way to reach his father's heart, all his efforts ended up futile. Finally, Vassili's father decided to take a new wife, a seamstress named Mariya. Vassili knew her to be a widow, as her husband died the same year as Larissa. He thought his father probably saw some sort of comfort in this kinship and he tried to be optimistic. Mariya was not only beautiful, she also had two older sons, Nikolai and Vladimir. Therefore, Vassili hoped that he would finally have someone to spend time with. This way, maybe they could at least fix some of the things torn apart with Larissa's death.

Alas, it wasn't meant to be. For all Mariya's beauty, she lacked Larissa's kindness and gentleness. When her husband was present, she pretended to care for Vassili, but when he left the house, she changed entirely.

Vassili never told his father anything, as he did not want his father to fall even deeper into despair. Even so, in spite of Mariya's efforts and Vassili's silence, Dimitri seemed to notice the problem. He started spending less and less time at home. Finally, after only a year of marriage with Mariya, Dimitri left for the big city, supposedly to sell his carvings. Vassili waited for him to come back, but as the months passed and his father did not return, he realized that Dimitri had decided to leave them. He wanted to be angry, but in truth, he felt too hurt that his father abandoned him to his fate.

In the midst of all the sadness, Vassili did have one light, the toy soldier his mother]left him. Whenever Mariya and her sons ordered him to do unreasonably hard tasks for his young age, he would retreat to his small room and feed the wooden doll a piece of bread and cheese. Just like that, the toy would come alive and help Vassili finish his difficult tasks.

Of course, it would have been easy for Vassili to allow his wooden friend to do everything for him. However, Larissa had not educated him to be idle, and so he always worked by his soldier friend's side, doing his best to finish at least a part of the chores Mariya gave.

Sometimes Vassili asked himself how his mother even managed to gift him with such a valuable treasure. However, he felt too afraid to ask, knowing that Mariya would probably punish him and take away the toy. As such, Vassili kept his mother's gift a secret. Even if Mariya or her sons saw the soldier, it seemed nothing more than a wooden toy. The soldier remained silent and lifeless to everyone but

Vassili, nothing but a harmless, old toy. Only Vassili knew that the soldier could actually do impossible tasks and lift incredibly heavy weights.

As the years passed, Vassili grew into a handsome young man. The girls in the village would turn their heads when he passed, giggled or sighed dreamily. They blushed when he smiled gently at them and offered to carry their heavy baskets. Sometimes they would bake him cookies and modestly send them to him with their thanks for all his help.

His stepbrothers weren't happy at all about Vassili's popularity. They sent their younger stepbrother to do the worst of the tasks around the house. Vassili knew they hoped that one day, he'd drop his axe and accidentally chop one of his limbs off. Perhaps the sun would burn his fair skin, or his body would suffer in consequence for all of the hard work. However, all their plotting failed. With the help of the toy soldier, Vassili managed to do all the tasks and foil all their plans.

This changed one dark autumn night. As usual, Vassili and his brothers silently worked in the chilly kitchen, each on their assigned tasks. Nikolai attempted to repair an old chair, while Vladimir sharpened knives. As usual, Vassili carved wood. He'd discovered that he inherited his father's talent to carve. Vassili knew his stepmother hated this reminder of her husband, but she still accepted Vassili's carving. His work was beautiful and earned them healthy sums of money.

Since Dimitri had left, Vassili's stepmother insisted on saving as much money as they could, so at dusk, they would leave only one candle burning. Given that they often worked with dangerous tools, it was unwise. Vassili refrained from pointing this out, for it would only earn him a beating.

Suddenly, Vassili heard a sound outside, echoing in the silent kitchen like an eerie omen. He looked up from his work to see a dark shadow pass through their courtyard. It seemed like the silhouette of a horseman, barely discernable, almost invisible in the darkness of the night. Just as Vassili got up to find out the identity of the intruder, the candle that shed light over the kitchen blew out.

Nikolai cursed and got up to look for something to relight the candle with. He slipped into the house where the fire still burned to keep the rooms warm. Vassili waited for his stepbrother to return, squirming when Vladimir glared at him as if the situation was somehow his fault. Finally, Nikolai reentered the kitchen, a glum look on his face.

"The fire in the stove is out as well. I tried lighting the candle using the embers, but it simply won't work."

Vladimir directed his glare toward Nikolai. "What do you mean it won't work? How hard can something like that be?"

"You try!" Nikolai snapped angrily. "I'm telling you, even as I light it, it flickers out."

Vladimir gave Nikolai a skeptical look, but didn't say anything else. Finally, Vassili realized it would be up to him to fix the situation. "I'll go ask someone in the village," he suggested. "Maybe they'll be able to help."

Vladimir turned toward Vassili once more and nodded. "We go together. God knows what stupid things you'll do. You're practically incapable of doing anything right."

Vassili suppressed the urge to counter his stepbrother's unfair insult. He pulled his own weight in their household. In fact, more often than not, he worked more than Vladimir and Nikolai. However, saying this would only get him in trouble. Therefore he remained silent.

Even so, he couldn't help but have a bad feeling about the whole thing. Taking advantage of a brief moment of inattention from his stepbrothers, Vassili slipped into the house, snatching a piece of bread from the table in the process. He heard his stepbrothers call after him, but he kept going until he got to his little room. Once there, he hastily found his toy soldier and wrapped it in a piece of quilt from his mother. He didn't have time to ask for advice. He'd take it along, just in case.

As Vassili got out of the room, he bumped into Nikolai. He let out a small awkward laugh. "Just got my coat."

His stepbrother grabbed Vassili's wrist and pulled him toward the exit. "Come on. We need to hurry."

Vassili winced as Nikolai dragged him along, squeezing his arm with brutal strength. He released his wrist from Nikolai's grip and followed his stepbrothers out of the cottage.

They walked down the path toward the village in silence, with only Vladimir making a few crude comments from time to time. Vassili hated being forced to withstand their company, but he could do nothing about it. He just walked behind them, ignoring Vladimir and focusing on anything else but his stepbrother's voice.

Finally, after what seemed like forever, they reached the village. Vassili noticed that just like their cottage, the other houses were shrouded in darkness. Vassili felt more and more thankful that he'd brought his toy soldier along.

Much to his shock, he realized a crowd of people swarmed the village center. They hastily approached and Vladimir stopped the first person he ran into. "What's going on?"

The other man gave Vladimir a slightly nervous look. "The light, it's gone. No one can light any candle or fires in their homes."

Murmurs started in the crowd, whispers of a curse falling over the village. The people started to panic and Vassili thought he could hear children crying.

Luckily, or unluckily, his stepbrother intervened to take control of the situation. "Calm down!" Vladimir shouted. "This isn't helping."

Nikolai nodded. "We need a solution. Weeping and bemoaning won't fix things."

"What solution?" the man they'd approached practically screeched. "Not even the priest knows how to deal with this. We've tried everything."

"I say we fight fire with fire." Vladimir's tone turned sly. "Someone has to go to ask for light from Baba Yaga. Her power would surely break the curse over the village."

Cold dread slipped into Vassili's bones. Only a few miles from the town center, the village path split in two and went on to reach a dark and mysterious forest. Everyone called it the Black Forest, because even on sunny days, it seemed gloomy, dangerous, and scary. Furthermore, dark whispers spoke of a terrible witch, Baba Yaga, inhabiting the Black Forest. Everybody knew that all those who entered the accursed forest were never heard from again. Baba Yaga did not take kindly to trespassers, and all those who dared to enter the forest ended up eaten by her.

Silence fell over the village center as the people contemplated Vladimir's suggestion. "Witchcraft?" the first man asked. "I don't know... Besides, who could possibly go to the Black Forest?"

"Vassili will go," Nikolai immediately replied. "He knows his way through those paths."

Vassili's eyes widened in horror as everyone turned toward him. He started to shake his head, hoping that the townspeople wouldn't force him into the Black Forest. However, as he opened his mouth to protest, a masculine voice suddenly sounded in his ear. *"Go, Vassili! Go to the forest. We are waiting for you."*

The voice sent shivers of pleasure down Vassili's spine. He almost gasped as his cock instantly hardened, as if obeying a command from the mysterious presence.

Feeling grateful for the darkness hiding his predicament, Vassili turned to find the source of the unexpected encouragements. Alas, even as the voice whispered endearments in his ear, his questing eyes couldn't find the person speaking.

Taking a deep breath, Vassili struggled to focus and offered the villagers a small smile. "All right. I'll go."

At that, the peculiar voice disappeared. Several people patted him on the back, congratulating him for his bravery. A few girls approached him, kissing him on the cheek and wishing him a safe return. Even the priest came forward, whispering a blessing. All the while, Vladimir and Nikolai just smirked smugly, and Vassili knew they thought he would be going to his death.

Vassili just ignored his stepbrothers. He thanked the villagers, although he wanted to smack them for their hypocrisy. Finally, when he couldn't take anymore of the smiles and well wishes, he turned on his heel and headed toward the Black Forest.

Chapter 2

The road from the village toward the woods wasn't easy, but Vassili was a strong young man and wasn't afraid of effort. In spite of the cold weather, his brisk step kept him warm. The moon shone brightly, and the wind whispered merry songs, playing with Vassili's long blond locks like a naughty tyke. It almost made Vassili forget about the horridness of his task.

However, all too soon, Vassili reached his destination. The Black Forest loomed ahead, looking even more silent and threatening at night. Vassili shuddered, feeling for the soldier in his pocket. He found comfort in its solid weight, knowing that his mother's eyes watched over him. Yes, she would protect him. He'd get through this, he just knew it. He still had his toy soldier, and as long as his mother's blessing supported him, Vassili could accomplish anything. Disregarding the feeling of dread that threatened to overwhelm him, Vassili continued walking along the path into the dark forest.

It was quiet, too quiet. Vassili knew from experience, for he spent a great part of his life outdoors, that nature was never silent. Birds chirped away, singing their own little ode to life. Sometimes crickets would announce the coming of a new rain that would feed their crops. Bees buzzed around in their hectic yet fascinating routine. If one paid attention, one could hear rabbits, deer, and all the other animals passing through the thicket. At night, the wolves howled their own song. There was always the sound of the river crashing against the rocks. In winter, when the river iced up and the rabbits hid in their boroughs, the wind would knock at the cottage's windows. Vassili sometimes imagined that the wind actually urged him to come out and play in the snow. Here in this forest there was nothing. Even the wind had gone silent, dead.

However, Vassili knew he could not turn back, not without the light for his stepbrothers. He walked in the eerily quiet forest, humming a merry tune to fill the unnatural silence. Vassili didn't know how long he walked through the undergrowth, when suddenly a horseman appeared. The horseman's face, his hair, and his skin were all as white as pure marble. He wore blindingly white clothing composed of a beautifully sewn white tunic and tight pants, complete with white riding gloves and boots. Even the horse was white.

The mysterious man glanced toward Vassili as he rode by. When the horseman offered Vassili a bright smile, Vassili resisted the urge to shelter his blue eyes at the almost blinding light. He wondered if he should strike up a conversation, maybe ask if he'd taken the right path to reach the witch's house. Before he could open his mouth, the horseman passed him by and disappeared into the foliage.

Vassili stared several minutes back into the place where he'd last seen the mysterious horseman. Something about the other man's smile had held him captive, frozen, and speechless. Shaking his head, he told himself to forget about the weird occurrence. Only then did he realize that dawn already bathed the world in daylight. Had he really walked for so long in the cursed forest?

Shuddering slightly, Vassili picked up the pace, knowing that he'd never hear the end of it if he didn't bring back the light from the witch. He walked and walked, stumbling over the numerous tree roots on the forest floor. He shielded his face with his hands when tree branches snapped at him, seemingly trying to stop his progress. Suddenly, a peculiar sight froze Vassili in his tracks. Yet another horseman. Everything about him was a fiery red, his flowing red braid, his clothes, even the pupils of his eyes and his horse. Much like the white horseman, the red one passed Vassili silently, but his lips twisted into a grin when he looked at Vassili's face.

As soon as the red horseman disappeared into the foliage, Vassili realized the sun now shone in the sky. Taking a deep breath, he struggled to compose himself. He wanted to get to the witch's house already, get the light and go back to his cottage. He most certainly did not want to think about the excitement he felt whenever the weird horsemen smiled at him. Focusing on his task, Vassili continued his journey toward Baba Yaga's house.

Finally, after wandering for countless hours, a cottage appeared in front of Vassili. It was surrounded by a fence made of human bones and decorated with human skulls. Vassili froze in horror and fright at the terrible sight.

In that moment, as if to complete the otherworldly spectacle, a third horseman appeared. His skin was black, he wore black clothing and rode a black horse. Vassili watched, fascinated as the horseman passed him by and vanished next to the gate of the house, but not before giving him a seductive grin.

The magic of the horseman's smile dissipated and Vassili once again realized his location. Night had fallen and the eyes of the skulls now shone like bright embers, casting an eerie light over the grove. Alas, he could no longer turn back. The earth started to shake and Vassili watched in horror as the witch entered the glade. She flew through the air in a stone mortar, using a pestle to guide her on her way and erasing her tracks with her ugly black broom. Vassili's eyes widened at the sight. The mortar actually looked like the one he used in their home to grind herbs. At the same time, though, it seemed so incredibly large and scary. The way the witch rode in it, crouched, her knees almost reaching her chin, only added to the unnatural, horrific spectacle.

Sniffing the air, the witch hissed in a raspy voice, "I smell a pure soul. Who dares to enter my domain?"

"It's just me, Vassili, *Babushka*," Vassili answered, unsure if addressing the witch with such familiarity was very wise. He hoped it would help him stay alive and uneaten. "My stepbrothers sent me to get some light from your beautiful cottage."

The witch examined Vassili with undisguised interest. "I will give you your light," she said chuckling, "but it will not be for free. You will receive a task. If you complete it, you will get what you came for. If not, I will eat you and your bones will join the others in my fence."

Vassili nodded numbly, too scared to speak again. Still grinning, the witch made a wide gesture with her pestle and the gate to the cottage opened. She pushed Vassili inside the courtyard, urging him toward the door of her house. Out of the blue, a black cat hissed at Vassili and a huge black dog lunged to bite.

"Away, you blasted beasts!" The witch waved her black broom around threateningly. "I am bringing him in. You will not hurt him!"

Just like that, the animals disappeared, melting back into the shadows they'd emerged from. Behind Vassili, the gates closed instantly with a loud bang.

Baba Yaga rubbed her bony hands in satisfaction. "As you can see, you cannot easily escape me," she cackled. "If you try to leave, the gates will not open. My cat will scratch and my dog will bite you. Now, for your task…Outside on the porch is a sack of peas mixed with poppy seed. By morning, you are to separate the two. If you do not succeed, you will be eaten."

After giving Vassili these instructions, the witch turned her back on Vassili and entered the cottage. Vassili sneaked a peek inside and watched Baba Yaga fall asleep almost instantly. He considered asking the help of his wooden friend but decided against it. What if the witch woke up? He would be in terrible trouble then.

Vassili took post on the porch, grabbed a rickety looking chair, and buried himself in the tedious task. He slaved all night long to separate the peas from the poppy seeds. Several times his eyes threatened to close, since his long journey had been incredibly tiresome. However, Vassili was nothing if not brave and persevered. He managed to clean the last of the peas just as dawn started to break.

Relieved at having finished his task, Vassili leaned against the closed door and sighed tiredly. A sudden noise startled him and his eyes flew open. There, in the witch's courtyard, the white horseman stood, smiling brightly.

"You are a very courageous and hardworking young man," the white horseman said and rode up to the porch. "Never change and always trust your heart."

Vassili gasped as the mysterious man gently caressed his cheek. Just like that, Vassili's fatigue disappeared and he felt refreshed, as if he'd spent the night sleeping and not cleaning a bag of peas. "Who—" he started to ask, but the horseman disappeared.

Before he could have time to contemplate this peculiarity, the door behind him opened and Baba Yaga emerged from the house.

"Are you finished with your task, Vassili?" the witch asked, her eyes sparkling with malice.

"Yes, *Babushka*. The task is done," Vassili answered, showing the witch the results of his work.

"Hmm...I am not convinced." Scowling at Vassili, the witch clapped her hands. Instantly, the black cat and the black dog padded to her side. "Tell me, my pets, is our guest speaking the truth? Or did he use some sort of trickery to deceive me?"

"He did it by himself, mistress," the cat said.

"It's true," the dog added. "We saw it with our own eyes."

The witch grimaced, obviously displeased that Vassili succeeded in finishing her task. Vassili inwardly breathed a sigh of relief upon realizing that had he asked for his friend's help, he would have been eaten.

"After I leave, you have to clean the house until it is spotless. Repair the roof and cook me dinner. After all this is finished, you will go to the barn and clean all the grain you find there of dirt. If you do not get everything finished until my arrival, *you* will be my dinner."

Terror gripped Vassili as the witch clutched his wrist with her bony hand. For a second, he actually thought that in spite of her words,

Baba Yaga would eat him. He felt her magic seep through him, making his mind fuzzy and weakening his body. Closing his eyes, he sent a prayer out to the heavens. *Please, God, make her leave! Help me!*

Much to his surprise, Baba Yaga let go of his wrist. Vassili didn't know if it had anything to do with his prayer, but he didn't really care that much. Chuckling darkly, the witch climbed in her mortar and disappeared into the darkness of the forest.

Immediately, Vassili dashed inside the kitchen and found some leftover bread. He could still feel her black magic surrounding him, threatening to consume him. He needed help. Taking his toy soldier out of his pocket, he gave it the bread.

"Oh, my dear friend! The witch gave me such a difficult task and she will eat me if I don't manage to finish it! What am I going to do?"

The toy soldier immediately came alive and ate the crust of bread. "Worry not, Vassili. Go work on cleaning the house and fixing the roof and let me worry about the rest!"

Yet again, Vassili obeyed his wooden friend. He found that fixing the roof of the cottage was easy for one as skilled in wood working as him. Still, he almost slipped and broke his leg when the familiar trot of a horse sounded in the courtyard. Vassili carefully climbed down to see that his new visitor was the red horseman from before.

The strange man gave Vassili a decidedly lecherous look and whistled. "You should have stayed up there," he said. "I had such a great view."

His expression sobering, the horseman gazed at Vassili with those peculiar red eyes. "Be careful, young Vassili. If you get in trouble, don't stand around and wait for her to eat you. There's a hole in the fence behind that tree. If something happens, take that route, run and don't look back."

Vassili nodded and opened his mouth to thank the strange horseman for his advice. He wasn't all that surprised when he didn't get the chance. The red horseman pressed a kiss to Vassili's forehead.

Just like his white counterpart, he then disappeared into thin air before Vassili's very eyes.

Vassili took a few minutes to recover from the entire thing. It wasn't that he felt surprised at the horseman's disappearance. He'd already understood that in the Black Forest, things that shouldn't happen were a common occurrence. Furthermore, he'd realized long ago that things existed that couldn't quite be explained. After all, he owned a hand-sized toy soldier coming to life and helping him lift heavy pieces of wood.

It was something else that bothered him, a sensation deep inside, like his body melted and his blood turned into liquid fire. His mind seemed clouded by a peculiar haze. It had been the same with the white horseman's caress. That time, the witch dissipated it with her appearance. Now, Vassili found himself unable to put it out of his mind.

However, Vassili was a practical young man. He soon managed to compose himself and finish repairing the roof with relative ease. Cooking was a bit of a problem, since he'd never been a particularly good cook. Even so, he followed the toy soldier's careful instructions. Soon enough, a pot of delicious stew cooked over the fire.

As he started to clean up the leftover ingredients for the stew, Vassili heard a miserable meow outside, followed by an echoing howl. Looking out the window, he saw the black cat and the black dog sitting by the window, their noses sniffing at the tantalizing aroma of the food coming from the house. Now in the daylight, he could see that they were practically only skin and bones.

"Oh, you poor things! How long has it been since you've eaten?"

Vassili considered the wisdom of what he was about to do. If the witch found out that he'd wasted her food on the animals, she'd be angry. However, he couldn't leave the poor cat and the dog to starve.

Decision made, he grabbed a thick piece of meat and hurriedly sliced it in two. He gave the smaller piece to the cat and the larger one to the dog. "I would give you more," he said mournfully, "but if the witch comes and realizes that I fed you, it'll be bad for all of us."

With that, Vassili resumed working on his task. While the food cooked, he decided to start cleaning around the place. He almost threw up when he realized human remains littered practically every corner of the cottage. He steeled himself, determined now more than ever to succeed in his task.

"Oh, my dear wooden friend," he addressed his toy soldier, again feeding it with a little piece of bread, "will we be able to get out of this mess?"

The toy didn't answer, and Vassili couldn't help but be confused. He froze when he realized the cat stared at him intently, its eerie feline gaze fixed on the toy soldier. In his despair and terror, he'd completely forgotten about the witch's interrogation of her pets. What was he going to do now?

"Worry not, Vassili," the cat said. "We will not tell her anything. The witch has never once given us a kind word in all the years we've been with her."

"You've been so kind to us." The dog actually wagged his tail when Vassili turned to him. "I would not bite the hand that fed me."

"Thank you, my friends." Vassili   leaned down to caress the cat's black fur and smiled when she started to purr. "I wish I could take you with me when I leave this place."

"Do not fret, Vassili." The dog gave him a sad look, those black eyes looking strangely human. "In this world, each person eventually gets what he deserves. We are only paying the price for our actions."

Vassili wanted to ask what the dog meant, but he didn't get the chance. "Come on, Vassili," the toy soldier said, while chomping down on the bread. "We still have work to do."

With a final pat for the two black animals, Vassili hastily resumed his tasks. He smiled happily when he realized that his toy soldier had taken care of the hardest part of the task, the grain.

"Thank you, dear friend," he said to the toy. "Yet again, you have saved me!"

Vassili didn't have time to enjoy the relative peace. The black horseman suddenly materialized out of thin air in front of the witch's house.

"Be careful," he whispered. "She is coming."

Chapter 3

Taking the horseman's advice, Vassili immediately hid the toy soldier in his pocket. The ground started to shake. Just as the day before, the witch appeared riding in her mortar, guiding it with her pestle and erasing her tracks with her black broom. Vassili waited patiently for Baba Yaga, smiling gently as the witch entered the courtyard. All the while, he tried to quiet down the whirlwind of terror he felt inside.

"Welcome back, *Babushka*," he began, feeling proud when his voice didn't shake.

The witch just glared at Vassili disdainfully, giving the house a critical look. "Are you done with your tasks, little boy?"

"Yes, *Babushka*. Everything is done."

The witch arched a brow, her eyes narrowing in suspicion. "Even the grain?" At Vassili's affirmative nod, the witch's frown deepened. Again, the witch clapped her hands, summoning the cat and dog to her side. "Is this true? Did he finish the task by himself or did he use some sort of trick?"

"It is true, mistress," the cat lied smoothly.

"He worked all day to finish your tasks," the dog confirmed.

Vassili mentally gave thanks for the help of the two animals. He hoped their reassurance would be enough for the witch. Alas, it wasn't meant to be.

"Traitorous fiends!" Baba Yaga snapped at the animals.

Time seemed to slow as the witch extended her hand and snatched the toy soldier from Vassili's pocket. "What's this then?"

"Just a memento from my mother," Vassili stuttered, but he knew he wasn't very convincing.

"You think I am stupid? I can feel the magic on this thing." Angrily, the witch stalked to the fireplace and threw the toy soldier inside. Vassili gasped as he saw his wooden toy being consumed by the fire. His mother's generous gift always supported him as a friend and loyal companion. Now, it was gone.

He didn't have time to ponder on the weight of his loss. Having disposed of the magic toy, the witch directed her attention toward Vassili. Oh, no! The witch would surely eat him now.

"Run!" the dog barked. "We will distract her."

Indeed, the next thing Vassili knew, the cat jumped at Baba Yaga, scratching at the witch's face and hissing angrily. The dog attacked as well, his sharp teeth digging into the dry flesh of the witch's leg. Vassili knew that the animals' attacks would not stall her for long.

Hating himself for leaving his friends behind, Vassili turned on his heel and ran toward the gate. He gasped out loud when the gates shut in his face, effectively blocking his exit.

It was then that Vassili remembered the red horseman's advice. He turned back from the gate and into the direction of the tree that guarded the entrance to the witch's courtyard. Behind the tree, he found a gap in the fence where several bones had somehow been displaced. Vassili swiftly slipped through the gap and started running. He could hear the witch climbing into her mortar to chase him. Remembering the horseman's advice, he didn't look back.

Suddenly, in front of him, the three horsemen appeared. Vassili stopped in his tracks, feeling lost and confused.

"Hello, Vassili," the trio said all at once.

It was too much for Vassili. "What's going on?" he practically shouted, his mind overwhelmed by the day's events. "Who are you? What happened back there?"

"The witch is our mistress," the white horseman answered sadly.

"But we will help you," the red horseman continued.

"If you do something for us," the horseman in black finished.

Vassili considered the words of the three horsemen. The fact that they served as the witch's slaves seemed suspicious. However, it wasn't as if he had much of a choice. After all, the horsemen helped him before. "What will you have me do?" he answered finally.

"To gain our freedom from the witch—"

"We need someone pure of heart—"

"To give us her, or his, innocence."

The three men answered.

Vassili blushed at the implication of the horsemen's words. "Wh-why do you need that?" he stammered.

"Only purity has the sufficient strength to counter malice." The white horseman gave Vassili a gentle look.

"We are cursed and only you can help us." The red horseman smiled, his eyes shining bright like embers.

"If you help us we promise you that you will receive great pleasure in return," the dark horseman purred.

With that promise, the three men got off their horses at the same time.

"I am Deni," the white horseman said softly against Vassili's right ear.

"I am Sonta," the red horseman whispered against his left ear.

"And I am Noci," the black horseman said against Vassili's mouth, just before taking his lips in a passionate kiss.

For a beautiful second, Vassili lost himself in the kiss. He broke away from Noci and gasped in a panic. "Wait! The witch. She is following me!"

"She cannot catch you here, *lubov moya*," Deni said, smiling gently, surprising Vassili with the endearment. "Can you not see where we are?"

Vassili took a look around. It seemed to him that they were still in the Black Forest. When he thought about it, though, there was something weird about it, something he couldn't quite put his finger on.

"We are Deni, Sonta, and Noci, Vassili. Daylight, Sun, and Night. We are outside of time now," Noci answered Vassili's unspoken question.

"Outside time? But how?" Vassili asked, astounded by the turn of events.

"Yes," Sonta assented with a nod. "Due to our natures, we cannot be in the same place at the same time without halting time."

Vassili gasped at the astounding notion. "That's not possible. Can you really stop time like that?"

"It would normally not be allowed," Noci said solemnly. Three identical expressions of gloom gripped the horsemen's handsome features.

"You see, *lubov moya*, we are angels, fallen from our place at God's side."

A distant expression came on Deni's face and his voice took on an even softer tone. "As angels, we had all the gifts of God. We were surrounded by light, beauty, and perfection."

"We had each other, all the seraphim and cherubim to keep us company. I suppose we were like brothers of sorts, although we didn't even have the comfort of having a blood bond between one another," Sonta said with a sigh. "Angels simply do not exist that way."

"Therefore, we were not happy, for everything seemed so cold and lonely. We could not feel anything beyond simple affection," Deni continued. "We needed real love, warmth, and passion."

"The witch came to us, promising that she would grant us our wish," Noci growled angrily. Vassili shuddered at the hatred he heard in the horseman's voice. "In our loneliness, we did not see her deception. We made a deal with her, thinking that it would not be hard to fulfill it with our powers."

Sonta gently touched the black horseman's arm, calming his erupting temper.

"And fulfill it we did," he said. "Alas, because of our rashness, God cast us out of the heavens. We were not worthy of them anymore. That is how we ended up damned, trapped into servitude."

"But we can be redeemed, if one of pure heart is willing to give us his love," Deni finished, a sad, yet hopeful smile on his face.

Vassili's eyes filled with tears at the story. Why would someone be punished for wanting love in their life? Wanting love was such a natural thing. True, they might have gone the wrong way to fulfill their wish, but did they really deserve eternal slavery for it?

"Oh, don't cry, Vassili!" Deni petted Vassili's hair comfortingly. "It's all right now. Everything is going to be all right."

Vassili wiped his tears, angry with himself for being so weak. "I want to help you, I really do. What do we do?"

Noci grinned wickedly, his eyes deep pools of alluring darkness. In two seconds flat, Vassili found himself stripped naked and flipped on all fours on the ground.

"So pure," Deni whispered against his lips, kissing him gently.

"So passionate," Sonta murmured, busying himself with licking a trail of fire on Vassili's back.

"So sexy," Noci purred from behind him.

Vassili trembled at the sudden onslaught of sensation that overloaded his senses. He wasn't afraid, not really. Somehow he knew that the three handsome horsemen would not hurt him. Still, he found comfort when Deni gently caressed his face.

"Hush. Don't be afraid," the white horseman whispered softly. "We'll go slow."

Vassili forgot all about the comforting words when he felt his body prodded from behind. An unfamiliar touch ghosted over his nether opening and Vassili let out a choked sound. The feeling of anticipation, the passion that sizzled in the air, everything was so peculiar and new. Even so, it wasn't just the novelty that felt scary. It was something else, something deep inside. He saw an emotion in his heart that hadn't been there before and that he couldn't even identify.

His thoughts evaporated when he felt his ass cheeks separated, his most hidden place exposed for everyone to see. He felt his face flame at the embarrassing position and fought to keep himself from tensing.

He didn't have to fight this battle for long. Deni slipped under his body and suddenly, wet heat engulfed Vassili's cock. Vassili's eyes opened wide at the incredible sensation. A needy moan escaped his lips. "Oh, God, Deni!"

He was so lost in the sensation he almost missed Noci's next words. "Open your mouth, *lubov moya*. Come on!"

Vassili obeyed, and he found himself with Sonta's cock teasing at his lips. He briefly hesitated, acknowledging his own inexperience. However, Noci continued to encourage him with soft, almost incomprehensible whispers in his ear. His insides burning, Vassili finally wrapped his lips around the swollen shaft. Alas, he couldn't really concentrate at all with Deni sucking him. Nevertheless, Sonta seemed to find pleasure in his inexperienced tongue. The red horseman groaned out loud as he started thrusting in and out of Vassili's mouth.

Just when he thought that surely nothing could enflame him further, Vassili felt a wet tongue teasing his entrance. Noci's tongue naughtily penetrated his passage, pushing in and out of his body, imitating an act as old as time itself. Vassili almost moaned in protest as the tongue retreated, but so many sensations took hold of him that he couldn't bring himself to do so.

And then all else faded, as Noci's cock replaced his tongue. The black horseman slowly started to push inside. Tears filled Vassili's eyes as Noci's invading cock painfully stretched his body. Even, in the sea of pleasure that surrounded him, the pain was almost welcome. It seemed like a spice in a sweet drink, complementing the cocktail perfectly. Vassili found himself impaled by a man's cock, while another man fucked his mouth, and yet another sucked him off. There was something so purely carnal and so out of this world in the whole experience that Vassili almost thought he'd fallen into a dream.

Noci started to thrust in and out of him, swiftly establishing an excruciating rhythm. Vassili gasped as the black horseman hit a magical spot inside of him, making stars dance in Vassili's vision. With every thrust that unerringly hit that spot, Vassili's pleasure increased exponentially. He moaned around Sonta's cock and felt the other man shudder as he tried to take in as much as he could from the red horseman's cock. He was surrounded by an onslaught of sensation, his entire body engulfed in a heat that threatened to consume him. They were no longer four different people brought together by a curse and a blessing. They became one entity, one soul, united in the intensity of their passion.

Vassili's mind soon became lost, lost in another world. He forgot everything he was, everything he had been. He only cared about the four of them locked in this intimate act together. It seemed as if he could feel all of them at once, three separate energies surrounding him with their surreal power.

Alas, all good things must come to an end, for Vassili soon felt the impending need to climax. Digging his nails into the ground and ripping the green grass, he tried to hold himself back. He did not want this to be over. He did not want to forgo Noci's power, Sonta's passion, and Deni's gentleness. He needed to live in this moment forever. Ironically, even if time had frozen for everybody else, he was still bound by it.

Obviously, the three horsemen felt the fire in his body. Sonta's hands gentled in his blond hair, turning into a careful yet teasing caress. Deni started sucking harder on his shaft as if he were trying to suck Vassili's brains out through his dick. The final blow came from Noci.

"That's it, *lubov moya*. Come! Come for us," Noci purred in his ear.

The seductive voice, the same whisper Vassili heard in the village pushed him over the brink. He came, bright lights exploding before his eyes. He felt the warmth of Noci's own orgasm fill him and tasted cum in his mouth as Sonta joined them in the peak of their pleasure. The knowledge that he'd also brought his lovers to their climax only increased his pleasure. For one moment, he thought that the intensity of his orgasm would make him black out. Thankfully, his body didn't betray him in such a manner. He managed to open his eyes and immediately turned toward Deni. "What about you?" he asked, feeling uncertain. Unlike with the other two horsemen, he wasn't sure Deni reached his peak.

"Don't worry, *lubov moya*," Deni answered him, a satisfied smile playing on his lips. "I came when you did."

"I would expect so." Noci chuckled. "He loves to suck cock."

Deni threw the black horseman a glare that would have withered trees. "You make me sound like a slut."

"You *are* a slut." Noci grinned, obviously reveling in the banter.

As the white and the black horseman started to bicker, Sonta winked, drawing Vassili's nude body toward him. "Let them argue. That way I get you all to myself."

The red horseman's words broke up the peculiar dispute. The other two horsemen turned twin glares of evil toward Sonta.

"Move over," Noci growled. Sonta obeyed without a word, seemingly very pleased at his ability to manipulate his two companions. Vassili suppressed a satisfied sigh when he found himself in the embrace of three very sexy men. Cuddling wasn't a very easy thing to do with four people involved, but somehow they made it work. Deni hugged Vassili from the front and Sonta spooned him from behind. Noci somehow ended up behind Sonta, his dark arm stretching over the red horseman's waist toward Vassili's.

"Sleep, *lubov moya*," Deni whispered, gently caressing his hair. "Rest now."

Lulled by the sound of Deni's voice, Vassili fell into a deep sleep.

Chapter 4

When Vassili opened his eyes, he realized he was alone. Instantly, he could tell that time once again flowed naturally, which meant one thing. The three horsemen were gone. When he looked around a bit more carefully, he realized he could hear the chirping of birds and the rush of a river nearby. His eyes widened as he realized that he no longer in the Black Forest but in a little grove just a mile away from his father's cottage.

He saw then that next to him, his wooden soldier waited patiently. And next to the toy soldier lay a skull, obviously taken from the witch's fence. Its eyes burned bright in the dim light of the evening. The horsemen had come through for him.

Vassili pocketed the toy and reluctantly took the skull. Using a branch to lift it up, he then took off with all speed toward the house. His steps swiftly led him through the paths he knew so well. He simply knew his stepmother and stepbrothers would give him hell for taking so long in getting the light.

In a few minutes, Vassili reached the house that long ago stopped being his home. He had barely opened the door when his step-family attacked him.

"What took you so long?" Vladimir snapped. "No one could light one candle in your absence."

"Stupid boy, how were we supposed to work without light?" Mariya hissed, glaring.

"You're useless!" Nikolai spat. "You've always been trying to break us apart and sabotage us."

Letting out a sound of anger, Nikolai lunged and punched Vassili in the face.

At the sudden hit, Vassili lost his balance, reaching out to steady himself against the kitchen table. However, in the process, the skull he'd been carrying dropped to the floor with a hollow sound. Then, the most terrifying thing happened. It eerily started to levitate, its burning eyes fixed on Vassili's stepbrothers and on Mariya. Before Vassili's terrified eyes, fire emerged from the skull's eyes, burning into the flesh of the three. The trio started to scream and lunged for the door, trying to make their escape from the skull's lethal gaze. It was futile. Wherever they went, the skull followed. The cottage filled with the stink of death and burnt flesh.

All the while, Vassili just stood there, frozen, terrified at the sounds of the screams and even more terrified when the screams stopped. His steps hesitantly carried him out of the kitchen and into the bedroom, where he saw the unrecognizable forms of what had been Mariya, Vladimir, and Nikolai. Before his very eyes, the charred bodies withered away and turned into ash.

Vassili screamed, the gruesome sight too much for him to bear. He never had a good relationship with them, but neither did he hate them or wish them ill. Tears flowing down his cheeks, he grabbed a shovel and went to the grove behind the house, the same grove where his dear mother had been buried. He put all his pain and loneliness in his work and struggled to dig faster. Finally, after much toil, a small, hidden grave awaited in the silent and cold ground.

He then hastened back to the kitchen and grabbed a clean pot. With trembling hands, Vassili struggled to gather the ashes of his dead step-family. Fighting to contain his tears, he carried them to their final resting place. He felt terrible for not being able to give them a proper burial, with a priest and a coffin. However, he could not tell the townspeople about the skull and what really happened with Baba Yaga. They would probably ask him to show them the accursed thing and God only knew what would happen then. Perhaps Vassili would end up with a whole village of burned people. He couldn't live with that.

With that in mind, Vassili took the skull and put it in the improvised grave. He whispered a prayer to the heavens and started covering the small hole.

When he finally finished, Vassili retreated back to the now cold and empty house, feeling numb inside. What would he do now? He had no one in this world. Bitter tears started to fall again as he remembered the three horsemen of the Black Forest. Where were they now? Had he really been so happy with them just hours before, or had it been only a dream?

He still needed to face the townspeople. Without the skull from Baba Yaga, he didn't know how to break the curse. He had no idea what to tell them, how to explain his family's absence.

As he stood there weeping on the porch, he heard the sound of a cart rolling past. It didn't really surprise him. Wagons sometimes chose this more remote path to avoid the hustle and bustle of the main road. Therefore, Vassili didn't even lift his eyes. In fact he wanted to run away, knowing that whoever was coming would probably ask him about his visit to the Black Forest. He barely suppressed his wince when an unknown voice suddenly addressed him. "What's wrong, child? Why are you crying?" An old man stood in front of the cottage, giving Vassili a concerned look.

Vassili bit his lip, wondering what he could possibly reply. "My family is gone, sir," he finally said. "I left to try and find light in the Black Forest and when I came back, they were just gone. I looked for them around the house, but to no avail. With the curse and all..."

The old man's eyes widened in alarm. "Couldn't they have gone to a friend or to a neighbor?"

"I don't know." Vassili sniffed, wiping at his tear-stained cheeks. "Maybe. I wanted to go ask in the village now, but I'm scared."

"Scared?" The man repeated. "Why, child?"

"I couldn't find the witch's cottage," Vassili cried, amazed at how easily the lies poured out of his mouth. "I couldn't help break the curse."

The old man rubbed his chin. "Don't worry about that, child. The curse vanished last night. Why don't we go look for your family now, all right?"

With that, the old man hastily gathered people from the village and started a search. Strangely enough, the townspeople didn't blame him for his inability to find Baba Yaga. Instead, they actually seemed genuinely repentant for having sent him there in the first place.

When their search bore no fruit, Vassili felt relieved but also guiltier than ever. As everyone said goodbye, sadness in their eyes, the old man gave Vassili a warm hug. "Poor child, all alone now. I'm alone as well. Come live with me!"

With tearful eyes, Vassili took in the figure of the old man. For all he knew, the man was a criminal or some sort of murderer. However, he had no one left in the world. What else could he do?

Therefore, Vassili agreed to the proposal. They left the house that bore so many sad memories and moved together into the old man's cottage.

Chapter 5

As the days passed, Vassili got more and more used to living there. He actually felt pleased for having made the decision. Even so, the memory of what he'd briefly had, and what he'd lost, still plagued him.

One day, Vassili chopped wood in front of the old man's cottage. His spirits were down, for even with the old man as company, he felt lonelier than ever. As he carried the logs inside the house, it occurred to him that whenever he felt lonely in the past, he started carving. Why not use it now to pass the time?

He sat down in the kitchen and retrieved a piece of wood that seemed smoother and of the right size. Taking a small pocket knife, Vassili started carving. He spent hours and hours working. When he finished he saw that the result was a beautiful carving of his three mysterious lovers. He wanted to cry at seeing the faces of Deni, Sonta, and Noci again, immortalized in wood by his own hand. He didn't get the chance. The door to the kitchen opened and the old man walked in.

"What are you doing, child?"

Vassili hid his tears from the old man, offering him a small smile. "Oh, nothing really. I'm done with the chores, so I'm just carving."

The old man looked at Vassili's handiwork and his eyes widened. "Child, you carved this?"

Vassili shrugged, not really wanting to see the portrait of his three lovers again. "If you think it's worth something, you can go ahead and sell it."

"No, child." The man shook his head. "This is too beautiful. It can only serve to adorn the king's hall."

With that, Vassili's old friend took the carved piece of wood, packing it carefully into a travel bag. Vassili felt thankful for the old man's idea. He didn't really want to see the carving anymore. It represented the clear proof of his hopeless infatuation and obsession with someone too high for him to reach. He couldn't help but feel that by now, the three horsemen had forgotten him already.

Vassili sighed, burying his face in his hands. At least it all served for a good cause. The three horsemen had been freed of the witch's curse. Surely that counted for something, right?

Trying to cheer himself up, Vassili got up from his chair and went out to stretch a bit. He'd been sitting down at the table where he'd carved for a long time and his back hurt. The sun still shone outside and Vassili smiled at it longingly. He reached out with his hand toward the sky, futilely trying to catch the rays. It was as hopeless as his obsession for the three horsemen. He was just a human. He could never hope to see them again.

Sighing, Vassili comforted himself with enjoying the sunlight. He closed his eyes and just relaxed, basking in the warmth of the sun. Suddenly Vassili felt ghost-like fingers caressing his face, a low voice whispering in his ear. His eyes instantly flew open, but his heart fell when he realized there was no one there. Inwardly sighing, Vassili abandoned his comfortable retreat, knowing that further lingering there would only torture him more. Taking into account the distance between the village and the big city, the old man would probably be gone for the night. Yet again, Vassili found himself alone in an empty house.

Vassili busied himself with finishing chores around the house, cleaning the chimney, dusting the little shelves, chopping more wood. He needed to feel the exhaustion of a hard day's work. Maybe that way, he would stop thinking about the three horsemen so much. It was unlikely, but he could try and he could hope.

Finally, when the crickets announced night had fallen, Vassili cooked himself a frugal dinner. He absently toyed with the food as he looked out the window and into the darkness that now shrouded the world. Would every single second of his life be like that from now on? Would dawn always remind him of Deni, the sun of Sonta, and nightfall of Noci? The natural flow of nature reminded him of the difference between him and his angel lovers. How could he possibly forget them?

It was so unfair. His life changed when he allowed Deni, Sonta, and Noci into his heart and mind. Still, he'd known from back in the Black Forest about the horsemen's divine nature. He shouldn't have let foolish emotions take over. He had no one to blame but himself for his pain.

Suddenly feeling angry with himself, Vassili abandoned his uneaten meal. He wanted to break something, take out his frustration on some inanimate object. Alas, he couldn't bring himself to destroy the old man's belongings. Instead, he hit the wall with his fist, hoping the physical pain would dull the emotional one. He wasn't some weak and frail maiden mourning the departure of her lover. He would get over the three horsemen if it was the last thing he did.

Naturally, the ache of his hand did nothing to help his situation. It only made him feel worse about the whole thing, more pathetic. Inwardly sighing, Vassili left the house he shared with the old man and headed toward the stream flowing nearby. He hated the fact that he had to go out and face the night. The fact remained that he needed to cool off his hurt hand somehow. Yet again, his own stupid temper and his idiotic heart forced him into a painful situation.

Having reached the stream, Vassili absently soothed his injured hand in the cold water. His thoughts wandered once more to his three lovers. He couldn't help but reach out with his other hand toward the sky, trying to grasp the elusive night. He wanted to scream when his touch only encountered thin air. He could do nothing, absolutely nothing to reach them.

Feeling defeated, Vassili curled against the trunk of a tree and closed his eyes. This summer, the weather helped the people and their crops. The sun became less scorching and the night kind and soothing. Sometimes, Vassili liked to think that his lovers had something to do with it. Then again, he'd become obsessed with them. His desperate infatuation probably made him capable of attributing to them things that could be easily explained by the whims of nature.

He lay there on the grass, bitterly laughing at his own stupidity and at the same time, yearning for the touch of his three lovers. The wind caressed his face, as if trying to soothe his broken heart. Vassili distantly recalled a different time when the wind had been his companion, the day of his sudden trip to the Black Forest.

A low whisper startled him from his contemplations. "Vassili?"

His eyes flew open, as they did every time when he thought he felt a phantom touch or the whisper of his name in his ear. He half expected it to be his imagination again, but this time it wasn't. Vassili's eyes widened as he took in the sight of three horsemen in front of him. Deni, Sonta, and Noci stood before him, smiling, as beautiful and perfect as ever.

Vassili didn't know what to say. As much as he wanted to see them, their sudden appearance stirred a whirlwind of emotions inside of him. He couldn't help but feel resentful for the fact that they abandoned him without a word. Indeed, they hadn't made any promises. Still, that night they'd spent together in the Black Forest had to mean something.

It was that anger and resentment that gave him the power to speak. "What are you doing here?" he asked, feeling proud that his voice showed nothing of his inner turmoil.

He knew he sounded snappish, as the three horsemen looked hurt at his tone. Sonta even took a step back and Noci's smile disappeared as if it had never been, his expression turning almost stony.

"We're here because you called to us," Deni replied softly, almost pleadingly.

"I called to you many times. Why come now?"

Noci sighed and rubbed his eyes in frustration. "I told you he would say that," he muttered under his breath.

"Well, of course I would say that!" Vassili snapped again. "What did you expect?"

"Vassili, *lubov moya*. We're truly sorry we couldn't reach you until now," Sonta said apologetically.

"In truth, we probably shouldn't have come in the first place." Deni bit his lip hesitantly. "You see, the curse has been lifted, but we've not been able to return to our place in the heavens."

Vassili froze at the sorrow in Deni's voice. "I don't understand. Back in the forest, you said—"

"Yes, I know we said that," Noci interrupted him. "But in the same way your love saved us from the witch, it is now holding us back, holding us here."

"You have to let us go, Vassili." Sonta's voice trembled. Vassili thought he would burst into tears.

"I don't understand. How do I let you go?"

Deni looked away, as if unable to meet Vassili's eyes. "You have to wish it. To honestly wish us to find our way back to the heavens."

"But I do!" Vassili gasped out in protest. "I've always wanted you to be saved."

"You also wanted us by your side. Don't deny it. You know in your heart it is true." Noci reached to cup Vassili's cheek, but stopped himself just before touching him.

Vassili opened his mouth to counter Noci's statement, but he realized doing so would be a lie. It was true. He never actually wanted them to go back to being angels. In his dreams, they remained by his side, holding him, kissing him, loving him forever.

His eyes filled with tears as he realized that in his own selfishness, he kept his lovers from fulfilling their dream. Even now, a little part of him couldn't help but be bitter at the knowledge that they would leave him behind with a broken heart. Still, it would be for the best.

His three horsemen belonged in the heavens where they could live forever, and watch over the world. Vassili belonged here, with his own people, where he would grow old and die. Then, one day, he would return to the earth God had crafted him from.

Taking a deep breath, Vassili poured all his love and pain in his heart into one phrase. "I wish for my angels to return to the heavens and be where they belong." It physically hurt to know that he would never be able to see them again, but they were angels and Vassili was human. They could not belong to one human alone, as they had to spread joy and welfare to the entirety of mankind. Vassili loved them, and for that reason, he would let them go.

Three identical smiles appeared on the faces of the horsemen. Vassili hesitantly smiled back, pleased that he'd been able to make them happy. He fully expected them to leave now that he'd released them. Instead, they walked closer, so close that Vassili could feel the warmth of their bodies through his clothes.

"We have one more night together. Let's make good use of it," Noci purred softly.

Not even waiting for his reply, Noci pressed his mouth to Vassili's, coaxing it open with his tongue. Closing his eyes, Vassili surrendered himself to the passion he felt to these men, no, these angels. His horsemen, the angels he loved so much. Soon, he would have to give them up, but he would have this last night with them.

He distantly felt his clothes removed, but it was so fast he didn't even have time to register it appropriately. Soon he found himself surrounded by three naked bodies. Three pairs of hands caressed his skin and deftly found all his sensitive spots. He leaned into the embrace of the person behind him, somehow identifying the other man as Sonta. It was quite peculiar really. He found that he could easily distinguish the particularities of each angel's touch, as if their hands and bodies spoke to him without words.

Feeling dazed, Vassili opened his eyes only to be met with Noci's wicked grin. He felt Deni's hands caress his legs and gently lift them up, the white horseman's lips pressing kisses down his slender torso. Sonta's tongue started playing with Vassili's ear, his teeth gently nibbling on the lobe and his hands wrapping around him to tweak his nipples. In perfect synchronization, Noci massaged Vassili's hard cock as he toyed with his testicles.

Lost in all the sensation, Vassili leaned against Sonta and allowed himself to become one with the pleasure. He wasn't satisfied with only receiving, however. He wanted to give as well. He wanted the horsemen to feel all the love he had for them, even if only for one night.

He gently pushed himself from Sonta's arms and smiled when he saw three confused expressions on the horsemen's faces.

"What's wrong?" Deni panted out.

"Nothing is wrong. I just wanted to give you the same pleasure you're giving me."

It suddenly occurred to Vassili that he had never seen his three angels touch each other like they touched him. The last time they made love, they all focused on Vassili. In truth, the way they unashamedly displayed their sexuality in each other's presence suggested they might have been intimate before. Additionally, Noci had said that Deni loved to suck cock. How else could he know that but from experience?

Feeling wicked, Vassili leaned back on the grass and reached to massage his cock. His lovers' eyes went wide as they watched him masturbate.

"What do you want, *lubov moya*?" Noci growled out. "Tell us."

"Touch each other. Touch each other like you do when I'm not around."

At Vassili's bold words, Deni blushed bright red, until his white skin could almost compare with Sonta's. Vassili suspected that the other two would have blushed as well had their skin not been red and black respectively. As it were, they just stood there, gaping at him in shock.

Unlike in the forest, it was Sonta who made the first move. He reached for Deni's white locks and pulled the white horseman in his embrace. The mouths of the two angels clashed together and they hungrily kissed, feasting on each other's lips.

Grinning wickedly, Noci knelt behind Deni and reached for the white horseman's ass. Vassili watched as the black horseman spread Deni's ass cheeks and licked across his crease, much like he had done with Vassili himself in the Black Forest. He didn't spend a lot of time preparing Deni, however. Much too soon, Noci thrust his hard cock into Deni's body, causing the white horseman to arch beautifully toward him.

No longer able to stand aside, Vassili crawled toward them on all fours and took Sonta's place in front of Deni. "Fuck me," he whispered to the white horseman.

Deni's already unfocused eyes went a little hazier and he nodded shakily.

"Let me prepare you," Sonta said, obviously realizing the white horseman would be unable to focus on Vassili with Noci fucking him energetically from behind.

Vassili found himself on all fours again, with Sonta eating his ass greedily. He seemed as skilled at it as Noci. By the time Sonta deemed Vassili ready, Vassili begged and pleaded, incoherent with lust.

Sonta positioned Vassili in front of Deni and the white horseman thrust his own hard cock into Vassili's welcoming passage. Even with the pleasure Noci obviously gave him, Deni still found the perfect angle to hit Vassili's prostate with each thrust. Moaning and gasping, Vassili blindly reached for Sonta, only to realize the red horseman was no longer in front of him. Then a particularly hard thrust hit Vassili's pleasure spot and he realized that Sonta had probably gone to fuck Noci. They moved together like an orchestrated symphony, with Vassili ending up fucked with the combined strength of three angels.

It didn't take long for Vassili to feel his peak approaching. "I'm coming!" he gasped out.

He regretted his words seconds later when Deni's hand wrapped around the base of his cock, holding him tightly and effectively stopping his orgasm.

Deni kept him on the brink until he felt he would go insane because of the overwhelming pleasure. "Please!" he begged. "Please, oh, God, please!"

The second Deni's hand disappeared from around his cock, Vassili came undone, his world exploding in a million colors. His ass tightened around Deni's cock and he felt the white horseman reach his own peak. Together, the four lovers collapsed on the grass, panting in exertion.

Vassili closed his eyes, cuddling into Deni's chest. He felt a gentle hand caress his hair and sighed in satisfaction.

"*Ya tebya lyublyu,*" three voices whispered from the darkness.

As he opened his mouth to reply an "I love you, too," another voice interrupted him. "Vassili! Vassili!"

Vassili's eyes flew open and he took in his surroundings in confusion. The stream, the tree, the old man's house in the distance. The sun was up and the birds chirped cheerfully around him. It had all been a dream.

Chapter 6

Fighting to keep his disappointment from crushing him, Vassili focused again on the voice that awakened him.

"Vassili! Vassili!" It was the old man, coming down the path in his carriage. "You'll never believe what happened."

"Calm down, *Dedushka*. What's the matter?"

"I took the carving into the city and went to the palace with it, like I said I would. When the prince saw it, he said he simply needed to meet the person who'd crafted such a beautiful piece. You've been invited to the palace."

Vassili's eyes widened. It was a great honor to be invited to the imperial palace and a special guest of the prince, no less. Still, the news the old man brought unsettled him. He had heard things about the prince, things that made Vassili's heart heavy. Supposedly, the prince was a regular heartbreaker. He spent half the time in random trysts with lovers both female and male and the other half finding creative methods to humiliate his no longer interesting toys. What if he decided to choose Vassili as his next target of interest?

Vassili hated the fact that the thought even crossed his mind. He wasn't an arrogant person. The only luxury he allowed himself was keeping his hair long. It had been in memory of his long dead mother, since he'd inherited her beautiful blond locks. Even so, he knew others considered him attractive.

Suddenly feeling very afraid, Vassili hastily stole a piece of gingerbread from the kitchen and retreated to his room. He placed it on the table and put his toy soldier next to it.

"Oh, my little friend," he whispered. "What will I do? What will I do if the prince finds me attractive? I simply cannot forget them. Even if it was only a dream, I cannot forget them."

The toy perked up and grabbed the piece of gingerbread Vassili offered, munching on it happily. "Go to the palace now, Vassili! All will be well. You only have to follow your heart."

Relief washed over Vassili at his friend's words. Perhaps the prince wouldn't like him. After all, Vassili was only a lowly peasant. Apparently realizing he'd managed to soothe Vassili's heart, the toy stilled, yet again turning into an unmoving and seemingly lifeless object. Feeling a bit better, Vassili started packing, as usual placing his wooden friend in his pocket.

After a few necessary preparations, Vassili and the old man left in the direction of the big city. As they traveled, Vassili simply forgot about their destination, his mind lost in the recollection of the night before. Had it really been just a dream? He didn't think so. He clearly remembered hitting the wall of the kitchen with his fist and now the pain had disappeared entirely. It could only be the work of his angels. Still, dream or no, he clearly needed to let the horsemen go. He would probably love them forever, but their place would never be at his side.

Even with the cart at their disposal, it took them a while to get to the city. The roads were busy and the horse still a bit tired from the trip the day before. Therefore, the hour turned late by the time Vassili finally reached the palace. Vassili debated finding a room at an inn and going to the palace in the morning. In the end, he decided asking the old man about it.

"No, child." The old man shook his head, seemingly horrified at the thought. "You need to go now. We have already made his highness wait long enough. Ask at the gate first. If the guard says that his highness is busy, only then will we find an inn to sleep."

Vassili inwardly sighed at the old man's advice. He already didn't feel comfortable visiting the prince in daylight. Visiting him at night seemed somehow even more dangerous. Then he heard a familiar voice purring in his ear, urging him on and encouraging him. His heart jumped even as sadness gripped it again. He knew better than to turn. He would find no one there. However, it didn't matter whether Noci spoke to him or not. Feeling that his lovers still watched over him gave Vassili the courage to walk on, obey, and visit the palace.

And so, Vassili bravely walked up to the palace gates. Soldiers dressed in beautifully adorned uniforms stopped him when he approached.

"Excuse me," Vassili began politely. "My name is Vassili. I was invited to the palace by the prince. Do you know if the prince can see me?"

The guard gave him one look and a knowing smile spread on his face. "Right this way, sir," he said almost mockingly. The gates opened and the guard led Vassili into the palace. Only after walking for a while did he realize that the old man had not followed him inside.

The guard led him to a room where he was bathed and given new clothes to wear. Apparently, it wouldn't be adequate for him to see the prince in his dusty, plain clothing. With every passing moment, Vassili's dread increased. All these preparations only furthered his fear of what would happen when the prince saw him.

After he finished preparing himself, the tall guard reappeared and led him down a winding corridor. Finally, the guard stopped in front of two imposing doors engraved with the symbol of the royal family. Vassili gulped, knowing he was seconds away from meeting the prince.

The guard politely knocked, announcing their presence. A noble, manly voice ushered him inside. "Yes, enter."

Opening the door, the guard stepped inside the room, bowed lowly and said, "Your Highness, your guest is here."

"Ah…perfect!" the prince replied. "Show him in!"

Vassili swallowed nervously as the guard showed him in. There, lounging on a comfortable-looking purple couch, was the prince.

Vassili bowed low, his long blond locks practically touching the carpeted floor and eyes lowered at all times. As a peasant, he knew that he could not address the prince until he'd been addressed first.

He waited like that for minutes, acutely aware of the prince's eyes scrutinizing him. Every passing second made him feel even more nervous and apprehensive. He almost jumped when he felt a presence at his side. A gentle hand urged his eyes to leave the floor and Vassili looked up at the prince's green eyes.

"Please, don't bow," the prince said, smiling welcomingly at Vassili and gesturing him forward. "You are a guest."

Vassili felt a blush paint his cheeks scarlet at the prince's smile. "Thank you, Your Highness. You honor me through your invitation."

"Not at all. I am very pleased to have you here." The prince grinned, his eyes twinkling mysteriously. "I have to say, I did not expect someone so young to be the creator of the beautiful carving."

Vassili looked down at the praise. The prince's words seemed neutral, but his tone was anything but. He managed to gather his bearings and formulate a reply.

"Thank you," he whispered, struggling not to wipe his sweaty palms against the expensive material of his new trousers. "My father taught me everything I know."

"How interesting." The prince pursed his lips and analyzed his fingers in obvious boredom. "You're a woodcarver then?"

Vassili nodded. "Yes, Your Highness."

"And how old are you exactly?"

Vassili swallowed in nervousness, feeling his dread increase. "Twenty winters, Your Highness."

The prince smiled at Vassili, reaching out to take his hand. "Now tell me, Vassili, how would you like to be my permanent guest here? I'm sure we can find a lot of common interests."

Vassili gaped at the sudden proposition. "I… Your Highness, I can't—"

Vassili didn't have the time to finish the phrase. He yelped as the prince's hands wandered unbidden on his body, squeezing his behind. The prince wrapped his arms around Vassili, drawing him closer and leaning forward to steal a kiss. It all happened so suddenly Vassili didn't even have the chance to oppose him.

Vassili felt his heart constrict at the prince's actions. He didn't want to be another of the prince's toys. In truth, even if the prince became serious about him, a fact which Vassili very much doubted, his own heart still belonged to the horsemen. Just the night before, he'd relived the perfect passion that united the four of them. Still, hadn't he just promised to let them go?

The prince was indeed a good kisser. His tongue licked across Vassili's lips, seducing, coaxing them open. Vassili wondered if perhaps, he could have a second chance to love with this man. For a brief moment, he actually considered it. The prince was human, so perhaps it could actually work. He was handsome, intelligent, and experienced. But, no, it wasn't an option. Vassili's body reacted to his skillful touch, and yet, Vassili felt nothing.

He found it amazingly easy to break away from the prince's passionate embrace. It simply wasn't the same. Even if the prince could offer him love and not only sex, Vassili wouldn't have said yes. Actually, even taking into account the prince's humanity, a gap still existed between the two of them. Vassili remained a lowly peasant, a poor woodcarver. Not that it mattered. His heart would forever belong to his angels.

Vassili prayed that what he was about to say wouldn't get him killed. "I'm sorry, Your Highness. I feel very flattered, but my heart is already spoken for," he said, struggling to keep his voice from trembling.

The prince's countenance changed instantly, his charming smile shifting into a furious expression. "Insolent whelp! You dare deny me? Guards!" he yelled. "Take him away!"

The doors immediately opened , and Vassili wondered if the guards waited there especially for the purpose of dragging him away and locking him down like a common criminal.

And so, Vassili found himself thrown in the palace dungeons, all alone and miserable. Unfortunately, upon changing his clothes, he'd stupidly left his toy soldier in his coat pocket. Therefore, he didn't even have the comfort of his wooden friend. Bitter tears filled Vassili's eyes. He wished that he could at least see Deni, Sonta, and Noci one last time before he died for his transgression. He vehemently pushed his selfish wish away. They were probably in the heavens now, at God's side, as they were meant to be.

Chapter 7

The next day came much too soon for Vassili's liking. The cell door opened, the rusty hinges squeaking eerily, announcing his impending doom. The palace guards roughly grabbed Vassili and dragged him out of the cell.

Outside, an angry mob gathered. The old man who had been his friend up until the day before spat in Vassili's face. "Ungrateful traitor!"

Similar shouts sounded and Vassili thought that if not for the guards, he would have surely been lynched by the furious people. How could they say things like that? Couldn't they understand that he could not betray his heart?

In that moment, Vassili knew that he'd made the right choice. He could have never lived with himself if he agreed to the prince's proposal. His heart belonged to the three mysterious horsemen. If fate decreed that his sin and his love for three men would mean his life, so be it. He refused to feel shame. His love was true and he knew that, if only for a few moments, the three angels felt the same for him.

The whispered words of love from the dream gave Vassili strength. Head held high, he walked into to the palace courtyard, where the gallows had already been erected. Strangely enough, the prince also appeared, watching the spectacle from a palace balcony. He was dressed in all his finery and gave Vassili a disdainful look.

"You can still repent, peasant," he said, voice thick with suggestion. "Take back your words, apologize, and you will be forgiven for your transgression."

Vassili knew all too well what apologizing would imply, and he couldn't allow it. He met the prince's eyes fearlessly, shaking his head. "I cannot, my prince. Even if the price for my love is my life, I will not falter. I would not be a traitor to my own heart."

Vassili thought he saw a glimmer of envy and perhaps respect in the prince's beautiful green eyes. The shadow of feeling vanished just as it had appeared, and those green orbs became cold again.

"So you will betray me then. Fine. It will be as you will it." The prince nodded toward the executioner. Vassili closed his eyes and he couldn't help but smile as he felt the same ghost-like fingers on his face. Maybe after his death, he would be reunited with his three lovers.

A sudden collective silence made Vassili open his eyes. A thrown stone hovered, frozen in the air, inches from his head.. The rope had tensed, apparently seconds away from sealing Vassili's fate. The executioner had frozen, not breathing, his hand still on the lever that meant Vassili's death. Time stopped. There, in the middle of the palace courtyard, stood Deni, Sonta, and Noci, all smiling brightly at Vassili.

"We're sorry, Vassili," Deni said.

"Only true love could save us from our curse, and you had yet to demonstrate your love," Sonta continued.

"But we would have never allowed you to get hurt," Noci finished gravely.

Together, the three men rode up to the gallows. The rope came undone and Vassili fell into Deni's embrace.

"I don't understand. You said I needed to let you go," Vassili replied, feeling confused.

"Oh, Vassili, we were forced to deceive you about that. You had to prove that you were willing to sacrifice yourself for us. Only true love can give a human the power of self-sacrifice. It was the one thing that could break the curse and return us to our place in the heavens," Deni explained.

"Please forgive us for hurting you," Sonta said. "We wouldn't have done it had there been any other way."

"We never doubted you." Noci's black eyes sparkled with affection. "We knew you truly loved us."

Vassili couldn't help but feel guilty upon remembering his one moment of doubt, the moment when he had almost yielded to the prince's attentions. He tensed and looked away as he realized that in truth, he didn't deserve the trust his horsemen placed in him.

He didn't know how transparent he'd been in his worries until Deni gently gripped his chin, forcing their eyes to meet.

"Don't worry about it," the white horseman whispered. "He is a handsome man."

"I have to admit that seeing you kiss him made me jealous," Noci said with a scowl. "Perhaps he needs to be taught a lesson in keeping his hands off other people's lovers."

"Shut up," Deni snapped. "We can't do that. We're still on probation. Besides, Vassili rejected him in the end."

Vassili couldn't help but feel both happy and extremely embarrassed at the conversation. His face flamed at the knowledge that his lovers saw him kiss the prince. At the same time, he rejoiced upon seeing them so openly jealous. They truly did love him. They loved him and came for him.

Again ignoring the minor argument taking place between Deni and Noci, Sonta smiled at Vassili. "Come with us now, please."

"But where will we go?" Vassili managed to ask. He could see them now, the wings attached to his lovers' backs. They were so beautiful it humbled Vassili.

"With God, the father of us all, of course," the red angel replied. "He is waiting. You will live outside time, with us."

Vassili could do nothing but nod in awe. So many nights he'd dreamed of this, dreamed of seeing his three lovers again. Even when he'd finally given them up, he still yearned for them. It was finally happening, his dream was coming true.

His agreement ended the fight between Deni and Noci as if by magic.

"That's wonderful," Noci purred. "I knew you would say yes. Besides, if you declined, we'd have found a way to convince you."

Vassili blushed at Noci's words. His blush vanished and turned into amused laughter when Deni kicked the black horseman in the shin and glared.

"Shut up! Really, can you two think of nothing but sex?"

"Nope!" Noci answered with a grin, ignoring Deni's anger.

Still glaring, Deni hoisted Vassili on his white horse. Before Vassili's astounded eyes, a portal appeared in the middle of the courtyard, just behind the gathering of onlookers. Just as they were about to enter the portal, Vassili heard the sound of a familiar voice. "Vassili, is that really you?"

Even after all this time, Vassili easily recognized his father. Placing a hand on Deni's arm, he urged the white horseman to stop. Noci helped him dismount as Vassili took in his father's image.

Vassili couldn't understand how Dimitri avoided being frozen in time like the rest of the people watching. He guessed it could be the blood they shared which allowed him to see his son for one last time. He wouldn't be surprised if his horsemen had something to do with it. It didn't really matter. Seeing his father in such a pathetic and weakened state broke Vassili's heart.

Dimitri had changed since he'd left the house. He'd lost a lot of weight, and his hair had turned gray, making him look older than he actually was. His eyes looked glazed, ancient, speaking of a sorrow he'd tried to drown in liquor. It was the same sorrow Vassili felt but had learned to live with. Dimitri's hands trembled as he leaned against the dirty wall, struggling to keep his balance. Those skilled hands, once so strong, barely managed to keep their grip on the filthy bricks. Instantly, Vassili knew that his father had lost everything, even the love for his craft.

Dimitri squinted as if he couldn't see very well and tried to walk toward Vassili, only to slip and fall back on the hard ground. Immediately, Vassili ran to his father's side, reaching to help him up. "Papa...oh, papa, what happened to you?"

Dimitri clumsily wrapped his arms around his son. "Oh, Vassili...I lost myself. I wanted to forget about everything, about all the pain and the suffering your mother's death brought me." He chuckled bitterly. "It didn't work."

His vision clouded by tears, Vassili turned to his angels. "Please, can you not help him?"

Deni didn't answer, hesitantly sharing a look with the other two angels.

"Why should we?" Noci asked, his voice holding a hint of resentment. "He abandoned you, left you alone with your stepmother. Why should we help him now?"

"Because I'm asking you to," Vassili snapped, unable to hold his temper. He loved his angels dearly, but he also cared about his father. Regardless of what Dimitri had done, he'd once been a wonderful father, a wonderful man. "And because everybody deserves a second chance," he finished softly, hoping the angels would understand him.

Noci just sighed and looked away. Following a sudden urge, Vassili took the black horseman's hand and kissed it. He realized Noci felt angry on his behalf. Still, he couldn't resent his father for loving Larissa with such an all-consuming passion.

"Yes, everybody deserves a second chance," Sonta said finally. "Carver Dimitri, step forward."

"What...who are you? What do you want?" Dimitri stuttered. "Are you angels? Am I dead?"

"You're not dead and this is your second chance," Deni explained. "Or a gift from your son, if you prefer."

The three angels lifted their hands and a kaleidoscope of colors surrounded Dimitri. Vassili watched in awe as the divine power of his angels healed his father, soothing his heart, giving him back the passion for his trade, granting him the strength to start over.

When the light died, Dimitri lost his pale and sickly complexion. The strong muscles he'd earned through his hard work were back and even his hair regained its color. The angels had given Dimitri the gift of youth.

Vassili smiled in gratitude at his lovers. Leaning over, he kissed his still-dazed father on the cheek. "Good-bye, Papa. Be happy."

Having said his goodbyes, Vassili allowed Deni to help him mount the white horse again.

He took another look at the frozen crowd, knowing that today he would leave them all behind. He didn't begrudge them for their cruelty. He didn't even hate the prince for sentencing him to death. It didn't matter anymore.

Suddenly, a thought occurred to him. He clutched Deni's hand in panic. "My toy soldier," he gasped out. "I can't leave it behind."

Noci and Sonta just chuckled. Vassili felt a bit hurt that his lovers would mock him. Granted, clinging to a toy might seem a bit childish, but the toy soldier was his friend and a memento from his mother. Surely, they understood that.

Just as Vassili wanted to launch himself in a scathing rant, Noci retrieved something from his pocket. Vassili gaped in shock. His toy soldier!

Noci ruffled his hair and brushed a kiss over his lips. "We wouldn't take it from you, *lubov moya.*"

"Besides," Deni whispered in his ear. "It is connected to us, just as our hearts are connected to yours."

Vassili opened his mouth to ask what Deni meant by that, but he didn't get the chance. A bright light surrounded them all, and the three horsemen of the Black Forest disappeared, carrying their human lover into the heavens that had birthed them.

Epilogue

Two beautifully carved crosses now stood in the grove behind Dimitri's cottage. The woodcarver smiled sadly at the inscription he himself had written.

"I am sorry, my love," he said softly, gently touching Larissa's name on the cross. "I have failed you. I did not know how to take care of my son. I hope he is happy, now that he is with you."

He'd seen it with his very eyes, the angels taking Vassili away on their winged horses. He'd heard Vassili's gentle voice plead for him, plead for a second chance for his wretched father. The angels had agreed. Dimitri now had his health, his skill, and even his youth back. Still, he would never have his family again.

Inexplicably, despite the fact that he'd seen the whole thing so clearly, everybody else missed it. They'd been shocked to suddenly see how the young prisoner vanished from the scaffold in the blink of an eye. It was probably the angels' work there. How else could Vassili have escaped being hanged like some common criminal?

Upon returning to his village, Dimitri realized that both his second wife and his stepsons mysteriously vanished in his absence. His neighbors could tell him nothing of their sudden disappearance, although since many of them heard of Vassili's sentence, they now blamed Dimitri's son for murdering them.

Dimitri knew that couldn't be true. His son was far too kind and generous to even think of something so horrendous. The disappearance of Mariya, Vladimir, and Nikolai would forever remain a mystery. Quite honestly, Dimitri could no longer bring himself to care about the three. The only thing that hurt him was the knowledge of how much his gentle son suffered with so much pain around him.

"Oh, my son, will you ever forgive me for abandoning you?" the woodcarver whispered, his eyes in tears.

A sudden blinding light appeared in the silent grove. When Dimitri looked up from the cross, he was astounded to see his beautiful Larissa, holding Vassili's hand. Behind them, the three angels stood, wide smiles on their perfectly sculpted faces.

"You are forgiven, my love," Larissa said in her musical voice. "Go and live your life! When it is your time, we will be here, waiting for you."

"Don't worry, Papa! I am happy now." Vassili beamed, his blue eyes shining so bright they seemed almost inhuman. A red arm wrapped around the youth's waist and he flushed, looking back at the trio of angels. "Stop it! Behave!"

The angel in white sighed tiredly and shook his head. "You have been given a second chance, carver Dimitri. We will be watching over you."

"Besides, technically speaking, you are our father-in-law," the black angel said cheekily.

Before Dimitri could fully grasp that peculiar notion, Vassili and Larissa stepped forward, giving him a tight hug. "Goodbye now, Papa. Be happy!"

Dimitri hugged his family back, his eyes filling with tears of both sorrow and joy. Vassili broke away from their embrace and for a second, Dimitri didn't understand his son's actions.

"He's giving us a private moment," Larissa whispered and she pressed her soft mouth to Dimitri's. There, in the grove where Larissa had been buried so many years ago, they shared another kiss, a kiss that no longer tasted like death, but like hope and promise.

"Good-bye, my love. I will wait for you forever," his wife said with a smile as their kiss broke.

"Maybe I'll come visit from time to time," Vassili told his father. "After all, I never died."

"Good-bye, carver Dimitri," the white angel said. "Until we meet again."

Dimitri watched, frozen, as Larissa took his son's hand. With a final wave of goodbye, the three angels, Vassili, and Larissa disappeared. The grove became as silent and empty as before. Dimitri would have thought it only a dream if not for the lingering taste of Larissa's kiss on his lips. As it were, when Dimitri abandoned the grove, he left his sorrow behind. In his heart he knew that both his son and his beautiful wife watched over him from the heavens. Perhaps he could not be with them now, but one day, when God willed it, they would be reunited. After all, true love lasts forever.

THE END

HTTP://SCARLETHYACINTH.WEBS.COM

Siren Publishing

Ménage Amour

FIRE
OF THE
FOUR SEASONS

SCARLET HYACINTH

FIRE OF THE FOUR SEASONS

SCARLET HYACINTH
Copyright © 2011

Prologue

Igor cracked his eyes open and made a grab for his blanket. By his side, his wife, Elga, lay cuddled, trying to find as much heat as possible. Winters were cruel in their land, and the fire must've died sometime during the night.

Resigning himself to the inevitable, he got out of the bed. He needed to rekindle the fire if he wanted to make the temperature inside their little home at least bearable. Thankfully, he'd retrieved logs the night before, and there were still some burning coals in the hearth. Soon, Igor had a merry fire crackling.

Igor stared into the bright flames, hypnotized by their dance. Sometimes, he imagined he could hear the flames murmur to him, or laugh gaily. Anyone else would have scorned him for his fancies, but his wife went along with it. She even said she heard the snow sing sometimes.

As if summoned by his thoughts, Elga appeared by his side. She smiled at him, and Igor's heart squeezed with love for her. With age, her face became lined and her hands calloused from a working life. Even so, her eyes still shone, like they did the day he'd met her.

"What are you doing, old man?" She shook her head and tsked at him. "Come and eat."

As Elga set the breakfast table, Igor scanned the two lonely seats with a heavy heart. The Goddess had not graced them with the miracle of children and, even if he'd waited and hoped, he'd pretty much given up by now. Both he and Elga were beginning to age, and his wife would no longer be able to bear children. Igor didn't fault her, though. He loved Elga, and she loved him. It simply hadn't been fated for them.

They sat down and thanked the Goddess for their meal. They weren't rich, but they weren't poor either. Igor just wished they could have left it all to a child.

All of a sudden, Elga threw a glance toward the window. "Look!" she exclaimed. "It's snowing."

Igor laughed. His wife loved snow. Admittedly, there was something about the beautiful, fluffy flakes that fell on a chilly winter morning. Their crystalline perfection and delicate uniqueness could charm even the hardest of men. But for Igor's part, he preferred the warmth of the fire to the winter cold.

It didn't surprise him, however, when Elga shot to her feet, abandoning her meal. "Let's go outside," she said. "I want to make a snow angel."

In that moment, she seemed so young and carefree Igor could deny her nothing. He nodded and after Elga cleaned up, they bundled up in their outerwear, ready to brave the chill. By the time they went outside, a thick layer of white already covered the ground. Igor guessed it must've snowed some during the night as well.

Elga laughed happily as she danced amongst the falling flakes. Igor just watched his wife, smiling when she plopped down in the snow and moved her arms and legs to create an angel. But alas, they weren't young anymore, and their bodies soon began to protest the abuse. They returned inside their home and took off their wet clothing. Afterwards, they sat together in front of the warm fire. "I wish we had someone to share this with," Elga said with a sigh, staring out the window. "I wish that, too," Igor replied, his gaze on the blazing fire.

* * * *

That night, Elga had a dream. She dreamt snowflakes danced toward her in a white whirlwind. She saw the snow angel she'd made and skipped toward it. As if in slow motion, the figure of the angel began to rise and slowly morph into a beautiful little girl.

Elga took the girl into her arms, carrying the child into the safety of their home. She caught sight of the burning fire and saw embers float away, sweeping through the air in a rain of light. They landed in front of her and materialized into the form of a young boy.

"Hello, Mama," the girl said, her voice crystal clear like the icy water of a river.

"Mama, I'm so happy to meet you," the boy said, his smile warm and kind.

Elga spoke to no one about her dream, but in her heart, she didn't feel surprised when, a few weeks later, their town doctor gave her and Igor the happy news that they would soon become parents.

Chapter 1

"Alexei! Alexei, where are you?"

Alexei lifted his eyes at the sound of his sister's voice. His hand slipped, and his hammer narrowly missed crushing his fingers. Cursing his own carelessness and Eva's bad timing, he called out, "In here. What is it?"

Eva peaked inside the room and scrunched up her nose. "Why must you be in such dirty places whenever I need you?" she asked. Today, she wore a beautiful blue outfit that complemented her azure gaze and white-blond hair to perfection, but as always, was far too light for the freezing weather outside.

"Because I have work to do," Alexei drawled out. He'd been slaving to fix the barn for the past few hours, but it didn't bother him. Taking into account the harsh weather outside, he'd allowed himself the luxury of a small torch here. As long as he didn't have to withstand the cold, he accepted whatever task his parents gave him.

Predictably, the torch prevented Eva from even coming inside. She enjoyed low temperatures, and often went out in the freezing cold with nothing more than a light dress on. But sun and fire seemed to scorch her. For this reason, she spent all of the sunny days inside in her room, which she always kept chilly. All the while, Alexei hated to go out in the cold. For this reason, Alexei had never been able to play with his twin outside or spend too much time with her at all.

Still standing in the doorway, she arched a brow at him. "Well, are you almost done?"

Alexei considered his reply. He didn't have much left to do, just to wrap things up here. But after that, he'd have liked to cuddle up in front of the fire, perhaps with a cup of mulled wine.

His decision was taken out of his hands when his father came in after Eva. "Ah, Alexei, my boy."

Igor looked around Alexei's handiwork and nodded. A feeling of pride swelled in Alexei's chest at his father's approval. "Excellent job. I know you're tired after this, but we need some goods from the market. Would you go fetch them?"

Alexei nodded, relieved. "This is what Eva wanted?" he asked, surprised. He'd expected something more unreasonable. His sister often frustrated him with her foolish, arrogant requests. Alexei loved her, regardless, and he did his best to comply whenever he could. They remained twins, after all, even if the similarities between them were few at best.

"Yes," Eva answered, "but I needed to tell you to get me some violets while you're out. My room looks so barren all of a sudden."

"Violets?" Alexei repeated in surprise. "In January? Can't it wait for a couple more months?" And since when did the barrenness of her room bother her? Eva always wanted things clean, spotless, and she didn't particularly like plant life of any kind.

Eva just smiled at him. "You'll do this for me, won't you, Alexei? I know merchants from different lands always bring flowers to the market."

Alexei's heart melted, and he nodded. Of course, his father agreed to Eva's request as well. How could he not? Eva was their little princess.

A few minutes later, armed with a shopping list and a purse of money, Alexei readied himself for departure. He'd cleaned up and changed his clothes. He'd also taken a weapon along, just in case bandits made their appearance. Alexei didn't fear them. In fact, he feared very little, with the exception of the cold, perhaps. He hated winter with a passion. Usually, he enjoyed going out, but with such chilly winds seemed to drive all life out of him. Still, his father had asked and Eva wanted her flowers, so he couldn't exactly refuse.

Alexei got on his horse and, bracing himself, rode off. Their home lay a good distance away from the village. They had a bit of land, which they cultivated when the weather allowed it. Neither he, nor Eva wanted for anything. It made for a good, comfortable life.

As he galloped, heavy snow fell around him, shielding his vision in a curtain of white. Alexei focused on his goal and steadied himself. He would not allow some harmless flakes to defeat him. The renewed determination brought a warm glow coursing through him, casting away the chill.

He reached the village without incident, and he set about to purchase the items his family needed. Spools of thread and fabric went in his bags first, then a perfume. Everything was for Eva, Alexei realized. Why had she even come to point out her need for violets?

Feeling irritated, Alexei finished his tasks and went about to seek the flowers. People gave him odd looks as he asked, but in the end, they told him he didn't have a chance of finding violets here. It seemed to be getting colder and colder, so Alexei resigned himself to failure. Eva would have to be satisfied with the rest of her presents.

However, upon his return, the first thing Eva asked about was the flowers. She met him in the hall of their home and gave him an anxious look. "Well, did you get them? Did you get the violets?"

Alexei shook his head. "I'm sorry, Eva. I didn't find them."

For a few seconds, they just stared at each other, then Eva rushed off. "Mama," Alexei heard her say in the next room, "he didn't buy me violets. I want my violets."

Alexei sighed, readying himself for a session of nagging. For whatever reason, Elga always preferred Eva over him. His mother stepped into the hall, a frown on her face. "I asked everyone," Alexei said before she could even begin. "There are no violets anywhere."

"Surely there's some other place you can look," Elga replied. "Go on now. You can't disappoint your sister."

Alexei desperately waited for his father to show up. Igor always took his side in these unreasonable debates. Alas, this time, Igor didn't make his appearance. "Well? What are you waiting for? Go," his mother insisted.

"But, Mama, where am I to find violets in January?" Alexei asked.

"Go to the forest," she suggested. "I hear there's a grove at the very edge. Folk say flowers grow sometimes, in spite of the cold."

Alexei gaped at her. How could she ask him to brave the icy winter through a peril-filled forest, all for a whim of his sister's? Did she not love him at all?

Disheartened, Alexei nodded and obeyed. What else could he do? When his mother decided something, no one but Igor could make her change her mind, and even Igor had a difficult time.

He set out one more time, this time riding in the opposite direction. He knew his way there well, as he often went to the forest to gather firewood or fruit. Of course, this was the first time he'd actually come here during winter.

At last, the forest loomed ahead. Alexei idly noted it looked very different than he remembered it. A few months back, its lush and verdant vegetation welcomed Alexei. Now, the leaves had all fallen, and just snow covered the trees.

Still, the woods provided a welcome change to the extent that the winds no longer beat Alexei so heavily. Acknowledging the treacherous path, he rode slower. He had no idea where he needed to go. Even if he knew these woods well, he'd never heard of the grove Elga mentioned. Other than the vague indications his mother had given him, he just followed his instinct and hoped for the best.

Onwards he went for the longest time. Finally, just as he started to consider returning home, he saw something ahead. A grove, just like his mother had said. Four tall standing stones rose in the center, the only change in the sea of white. Alexei could see no flowers, no violets, nothing. His tiredness turned into sheer hopelessness, and a heavy chill started to take over his limbs.

His eyes began to close, and Alexei struggled against the weariness. Unavoidably, he lost the battle, and his grip on the horse's reins. He slipped off the animal, and expected falling into the snow, perhaps to his death. Instead, he fell into someone's arms. "Easy there, young man," a male voice said. "Be careful."

Alexei's vision swam for a few seconds, but as the dizziness faded, the sight that met his eyes shocked him beyond belief. The man holding him had hair as white as the pure snow and icy blue eyes, just like Eva. The resemblances stopped there, as Alexei felt a very strong and warm male body against him. The chill ran off as if it had never been, replaced by pure heat.

"What are you doing here?" another voice said. Alexei looked over his rescuer's shoulder and caught sight of a second man. Alexei couldn't be certain, but he thought his eyes and hair were green as grass. Who in the world had green hair? The second man lay reclining against one of the stones, his gaze filled with a peculiar warmth.

To Alexei's surprise, he realized two other men waited in similar positions. The third one gave Alexei an amused look, his bright blond hair and amber eyes seeming to shine in the wane light. "I'm guessing his sister is being troublesome again. Isn't that right, Alexei?"

At last, Alexei found his voice. "How do you know my name? And how do you know about Eva?"

The fourth man chuckled, brushing his red hair of his face. His penetrating brown gaze analyzed Alexei with interest. "We know many things."

Freaked out, Alexei began to struggle in his captor's hold. The white-haired man released him, and Alexei immediately felt the loss. He struggled not to let it show and found refuge next to his horse. "Who are you people? What do you want?"

"I believe we asked you that first," the white-haired man said. "But since we do have the advantage of knowing your identity, we'll introduce ourselves. I'm Zimah."

The second man got up and bowed courteously. "Visnah."

The blond also shot to his feet and began to head toward Alexei. "Lyetah."

"And I am Ohsyn," the last man said, also making his way to Alexei. "Now, can you answer the question?"

Alexei realized he was being very rude. After all, these men most likely saved him from death. Clearly, they weren't common people. He didn't know if they were pulling his leg with those names, since he'd never known anyone called "spring," "summer," "autumn," and "winter." But at this point, anything was possible. And Alexei found he felt safe here, in this grove, just talking with these strange men.

"Eva wanted violets," he replied. "I couldn't find any at the market, so my mother sent me out here. She said there's a place where flowers grow in spite of it being winter."

Zimah hummed, sounding thoughtful. "Time is this way for a reason," he answered. "Can't she wait?"

"Apparently not," Alexei replied.

Visnah smiled at him. "Well, we can provide the violets easily enough."

"But on one condition," Zimah added.

"What condition?" Alexei inquired, almost afraid to ask.

"Nothing much," Zimah replied. "We just require a kiss, one for Visnah and one for me."

Alexei blanched at Zimah's reply. "B–but… That's not right." He shook his head fiercely. He couldn't do such a thing. For one, they were all male. Not only that, but kissing both of them also went way beyond what Alexei had ever imagined he'd do.

Visnah looked saddened. "Do you find the thought so repulsive?"

The fearful part inside Alexei wanted to say yes, but he knew it would be a lie. He'd long ago acknowledged his attraction for both males and females. But sodomy was supposed to be a perversion. He didn't know if he could accept the thing he'd struggled against ever since he'd first discovered sexuality.

And yet, he found himself shaking his head. "That's not it. I just... I don't know about this."

"It's just a kiss," Visnah coaxed. "Well, two."

Alexei looked at Zimah, then at Visnah, and couldn't help a wave of want. After all, what would it hurt? Eva would get her flowers, and Alexei would experience something incredible. For he had no doubt kissing either of these men would be unbelievable. "All right," he answered. "I'll do it."

Zimah gave him an unreadable look. "Excellent," he said. Zimah blew into the air and the snow around them began to dissipate. Then Visnah bowed his head toward the ground and waved his hand toward it. Flowers bloomed all around them, turning the forest into a green paradise. Violets flourished everywhere, and for a few moments Alexei was too stunned to even move. "Go on," Lyetah urged him. "Pick your flowers."

Alexei rushed to do as Lyetah told him. With trembling hands, he picked a bouquet of the lovely blossoms, caressing the soft petals. When he finished, he wrapped them in a soft cloth and placed them in the saddlebag.

This all seemed so surreal. Who were these men? Did he really run into the seasons themselves? No, it couldn't be. Witchcraft, then? Either that or this was some sort of weird dream. Perhaps Alexei had fallen into the snow and now hallucinated beautiful men.

Zimah's voice pushed aside his fears. "Now, our reward," he said.

Alexei nodded. His heart thundered as he approached Zimah and pressed his mouth to Zimah's in a chaste kiss. He'd only ever tried this with women, but he found Zimah's lips to be even softer than any maiden's. But Zimah was unlike anyone Alexei had ever touched before, and the man soon proceeded to prove it to Alexei. His tongue demanded entrance, and Alexei gladly complied, moaning as he did so. Their kiss reminded Alexei of a winter storm, not cold, but wicked, harsh, and unforgiving. Zimah took what he wanted, and his skin, strangely cold to the touch, seemed to warm under Alexei's touch. Alexei felt odd, as if the fire he'd always felt within him urged him onwards, to melt away the ice inside Zimah.

All too soon, they broke apart, with both of them panting hard. The other three men gave them heated looks. Visnah approached and took Alexei in his arms. "My turn."

Visnah's kiss turned out to be gentle where Zimah's had been rough and ravishing. He coaxed Alexei to relax, licking at the seams of Alexei's lips with excruciating patience. Visnah smelled like the fresh flowers he'd summoned, and a sense of tamed desire filled Alexei. He wanted to lose himself in Visnah's scent and taste forever, to enjoy the reviving energy that seemed to course through his veins when they touched.

When the need to breathe forced them to separate, Alexei stumbled away from the two men, his head whirling with arousal and confusion. Ohsyn caught him before he fell. "Careful now. We wouldn't want you to fall."

Alexei stared at the man blankly. "Do you want a kiss, too?" he blurted out.

His face flamed when Ohsyn grinned at him. "It wouldn't hurt, but Lyetah and I didn't help you, so we can't ask that."

Lyetah chuckled huskily. "But since you're offering, we won't say no."

Before Alexei could protest, Ohsyn and Lyetah kissed his cheeks. They should have been friendly pecks and nothing more, but with Lyetah groping Alexei's ass, they became something entirely different, a promise for more.

Finally, the four men urged Alexei off. "Go on," Ohsyn said. "Go home. Your family must be worried by now."

Alexei nodded. "Thank you for your help," he said.

He retrieved the flowers from the saddlebag and held them carefully while he mounted the horse. He didn't want to squash the gentle buds, and he needed to keep them away from the chill wind as well.

"Don't worry," Visnah said. "They'll keep until you get home."

Alexei waved at the four men and rode away. He forced himself to keep looking forward, but with each passing second, his heart became heavier. He found he didn't want to leave the grove. He wanted to stay here, know these men, talk to them, and find out how they knew Alexei, and why they'd helped him. Perhaps there would even be more kisses.

Alexei turned around and threw a gaze in the direction of the grove. He saw the large four stones, silent, and no sign of the four men.

Alexei would have thought it had all been a dream if not for the bouquet of violets he still clutched against his chest. Even so, he remained rooted on the spot, staring at the grove in hopes that he'd see the men reemerge. They never did, and when night began to fall, Alexei had no choice but to leave.

He didn't even know how he managed to make the trip back. It must've been the horse's instinct that kept him from losing his way. When at last he reached their home, he'd begun to doubt his own sanity. He kept an almost punishing grip on the flowers, expecting them to disappear into thin air any moment now.

The front door of their house burst open, and his father rushed out. "Come inside, Alexei. Hurry. I was just about to go looking for you."

Igor pulled Alexei into the warmth of their home. Almost instantly, Alexei felt better, the fire in the hearth calling out to him. Sometimes, he thought he could hear the fire speaking to him, whispering words of comfort and praise. *"Welcome home, Alexei,"* it said this time. Once, the cheerful greeting would have been enough. Now, Alexei would have preferred an explanation.

He took off his heavy jacket, carefully handling the violets as he did so. "Where's Eva?" he asked his father.

Igor's expression darkened. "In her room with your mother."

He seemed to want to say something else, but then, Eva burst in, bouncing toward him. "Well? Did you find them?"

"I did," Alexei answered. He gripped the violets in his hand, caressing the buds gently.

"Oh, they're so beautiful," Eva said. "Come, give them to me."

Alexei took in his twin's demanding expression. He realized he didn't want to give her the flowers. Sure, she'd been the one to demand them in the first place, but Alexei had witnessed the magical act through which they'd been created. He didn't want to let them go. He wanted to keep the tiny piece of the dream he'd experienced for himself.

But his mother came into the room, and Alexei knew he would not be allowed to keep the flowers. It would look odd anyway. Men were not supposed to get clingy over a bunch of violets. Then again, men didn't kiss other men either.

Eva's voice snapped him out of his trance. "Why are your lips swollen?" she asked, peering at him.

On impulse, Alexei covered his mouth with his hand. The action merely made Eva arch a brow and Elga frown. Alexei did his best to cover his suspicious demeanor with a nonchalant shrug. "Must be because of the cold."

Elga didn't look very convinced, but obviously, she couldn't find another explanation. "Give the violets to Eva," she said without preamble.

Helpless, Alexei handed the flowers to his sister. Eva squeezed them to her chest, making Alexei wince when the action hurt the violets. Elga, however, just kissed Eva's cheek. "Beautiful flowers, darling. Now run along. You should go place them in water."

With one graceful twirl, Eva took off in a cloud of perfume. Elga finally directed her gaze toward Alexei. "Well, it seems you managed to find them in the end. Where there's a will, there's a way."

Alexei bit his lip, barely managing to keep himself from crying out at the injustice. At least she could show some concern, given that he'd have frozen to death in the wild if not for the four men he'd run into. "Where did you get them?" Igor asked. "It's not the season for such beautiful flowers."

"Mama said there's a grove at the edge of the forest where they grow in spite of the weather. I wandered around until I found it."

Igor looked thoughtful. "Well, you shouldn't have gone. It's dangerous to go out in this freezing cold. And there might be beasts out there."

For a few seconds, something shifted inside Elga's eyes, like an unreadable emotion. But then, it vanished as soon as it appeared. "I'm sure Alexei can handle it," she said, shrugging.

"Thank you for trusting me, Mama," Alexei answered, keeping his voice level and respectful. At this point, he couldn't do much else. And besides, as much as the situation frustrated him, he remembered meeting the four mysterious men, and he didn't feel so abandoned anymore.

"Go on to your room and change," Igor said. "Your mother will have dinner ready soon, and then you can sleep for a while. You've had a very busy day."

Alexei took his father's advice, forgoing the call of the fire for the benefit of solitude. As he went past Eva's room, he heard her hum a low song, her crystalline voice reminding him of the sound of bells. Shaking himself, he entered his own chamber, locked the door, and took off his wet clothing.

He was supposed to get ready for dinner, but he had some time until his parents called him. Naked, he plopped on the bed and covered himself with the blankets. It felt chilly inside the bedroom, but the heavy quilts provided him with a warm cocoon. He'd have to start a new fire in the hearth, but he didn't have the energy now. Instead, he reached down to cup himself, leisurely moving his hand up and down his cock. A part of him would have preferred to imagine a beautiful woman while doing so, but instead, the four men he'd just met appeared. Alexei remembered Zimah's hot kiss and Visnah's gentleness, the promise in Lyetah and Ohsyn's touches. He wanted more. He imagined Zimah's kiss go on and on, never stopping. Visnah took position behind Alexei and began to caress his sides, reaching between him and Visnah to tweak his nipples. And then, when he broke away from the two, Lyetah and Ohsyn came forth. Lyetah knelt in front of Alexei, taking Alexei's prick in his hot mouth. All the while, Ohsyn reached between Alexei's ass cheeks, prodding at the hidden hole. One finger penetrated Alexei's forbidden passage. Alexei's eyes greedily took in the sinful sight of the four men in front of him. Zimah and Visnah lay together, their hands moving on each other's cocks as they watched Lyetah and Ohsyn work Alexei. Lyetah continued to bob his head up and down Alexei's shaft. And then Ohsyn's finger hit something deep inside him that made the flame inside Alexei spark into infinite life. He cried out as he found his peak, his orgasm sweeping through him stronger and brighter than anything he'd ever experienced.

Alexei tried to cling to his men, but they melted, and when the haze of the orgasm dissipated, they disappeared entirely. As he recovered, Alexei realized they'd never been there. His own fingers had massaged his shaft and penetrated his ass.

Alexei felt himself flush in shamed pleasure. He needed to clean up quickly and find a way to get rid of the evidence on the covers. It would be embarrassing if his mother found them. Hastily, Alexei rushed to his task. In a distant thought, he wished this hadn't been a dream, but reality.

Chapter 2

The violets didn't last long in Eva's room. The following day, Alexei saw her throw away the wilted, dried up flowers, and he sighed. He'd have liked to keep them. In his heart, he'd known his sister's whims would destroy the beauty of the violets.

No one made any comment on this, however, not even Eva herself. Elga laughed gaily as Eva went outside to play in the snow. For Alexei's part, he had work to do. He always did. He helped their mother with their animals who needed even more care because of the winter, then went out to get more firewood. He didn't mind. It kept his mind busy and away from other, more dangerous and sinful things.

At lunch, Elga cooked a hot meal, but as delicious as his mother's dishes always were, Alexei didn't taste much of it. He ate without paying attention, his thoughts unerringly wandering to the meeting the day before.

Yet again, Eva's voice snapped him out of his reverie. "Did you hear what I said, Alexei?"

Alexei blinked in confusion. "I'm sorry, no."

Eva sighed in something akin to exasperation. "I said the stew tastes excellent," she replied.

Alexei nodded, uncertain why Eva would have addressed this comment to him. "It does, indeed. Like always."

He meant it as a compliment for his mother, but Elga ignored him. Eva continued to speak, offering him a light grin. "And it would work great with a delicious dessert. I'm thinking strawberries would match the taste perfectly. Don't you agree, Mama?"

Elga smiled at her. "Of course, dear. You always grasp the essence of each meal. I'm flattered. Alexei, you should go to the market and get us some strawberries."

Alexei gaped at his mother. He knew for a fact he wouldn't find any berries there. They were rare even at summertime, and it would be impossible for them to appear in winter in the village. "Mama, there aren't any. I looked through all the market yesterday. I'd have seen them."

"Perhaps you missed them," Elga insisted.

"Besides, if you don't find them at the market, you can always go to the grove where you got the flowers," Eva added.

Igor looked upset. "Eva, you can have another dessert. Your mother just baked a pie. You don't need strawberries. Your brother is needed here, not to go wandering in the wilderness."

Eva's eyes filled with tears. "But, Papa, Alexei got the violets with no trouble. He'd surely manage to do so with strawberries as well."

Alexei wanted to scream. Eva just wept when she didn't get her way. Her tears unerringly made Elga angry. "What is the problem?" their mother said. "It is only some strawberries. How hard can it be?"

"Have you looked outside today?" Igor shot back. "The violets were bad enough. Now you want strawberries, too? No. I won't risk my son."

Alexei felt a bit better at his father's words. At least Igor loved him. However, the conflict was escalating, Eva's sobs fueling Elga's temper, while Igor refused to budge from his decision.

Alexei remembered the four men. Perhaps he could use this as an excuse to see them again. And besides, he hated the rare occasions when his parents fought, more so when Elga's disregard for him was the reason. He didn't want to be a burden for their family.

"I will go," he said. "Eva is right. If I don't find them in the market, I'll try at the grove once again. Perhaps I'll be in luck."

Igor turned toward him. "Are you certain, son? It's awfully cold outside."

Alexei knew that, but he counted on something in particular to warm him. His own desire sparked a fire within him, something that refused to go away no matter what and summoned him toward the forest. He'd have probably gone anyway, even if Eva hadn't asked for strawberries. "I'll be fine," he told his father.

"Then it's settled," Eva said, tears gone in an instant. "Oh, I can't wait. I've got a craving for them like you can't believe."

She didn't thank him, nor did she tell him to have a safe trip. And so, after lunch, Alexei was off once more. He'd have gone directly to the forest since he very much doubted he'd find the troublesome fruit at the market. In fact, he knew he wouldn't, but he didn't want to take the four men's help for granted, not when he hadn't exhausted all other options.

His renewed sense of purpose helped him during his trip in the cold, but once he got to the market, he began to regret his scrupulous decision. There were just so many stalls, and Alexei wanted to get out of there already and head toward the forest. Still, he clung to the original plan and asked every greengrocer in the area for strawberries. Predictably, they shook his head at his request. Some of them even laughed and pointed at the cloudy sky.

At last, after a frustrating and even humiliating few hours spent in the village, Alexei headed back. He rode past their home and took the same path he'd used the day before. This time, the woods didn't seem so gloomy and unwelcoming. In fact, they looked magical and mysterious, and Alexei entered them with excitement and nervousness.

Alexei did his best to recall the way he'd gone to get to the grove, but he'd told his mother the truth about "just wandering." He did have a general clue on how to reach to his destination, and his sense of orientation did help. Even so, it took him far too long to find the grove with the four standing stones.

At first, Alexei thought the men weren't there. He sighed and rubbed his eyes, weary after the trip through the cold. When he looked up again, he gaped, realizing his four dream lovers had appeared. "Well, well," Ohsyn said, "if it isn't young Alexei again. What is it now?"

Alexei got off the horse and greeted the men with a shy wave. "Uh… Strawberries. Eva wants strawberries."

"It is not the season for such fruit," Zimah pointed out with a frown.

Lyetah wrapped an arm around Zimah's shoulder. "But no worries, we can get you your strawberries. Isn't that right, Zimah?"

Zimah sighed and nodded. Lyetah grinned, his amber gaze sweeping over Alexei like a physical caress. "But we want our reward."

Alexei leaned against his horse, his legs unsteady. "Kissing again?" he asked.

"Just one this time," Lyetah answered. "For me."

Of course, Alexei agreed. Just like the day before, Zimah blew into the air and the snow in the grove vanished. When Zimah finished his task, Lyetah stepped forward. He extended his arms wide. Light emanated from his fingertips, turning Alexei's entire world into gold. When the blinding rays began to dim, Alexei realized the grove had turned blood red with beautiful, ripe strawberries.

"Go ahead and pick them," Lyetah said. Alexei obeyed, picking a reasonable quantity of berries. He didn't want to be greedy either, so he didn't take much. Eva's whim would soon be gone anyway, and it would be a pity if they spoiled.

"Now, for my reward," Lyetah said. Alexei licked his lips. He'd dreamed about this, wanted it since yesterday. He ached for a real kiss with Lyetah. It might have been wrong, but Alexei couldn't deny his desire.

He stepped forward toward the blond, gulping. Lyetah picked a ripe berry and held it to Alexei. The gesture felt so undeniably intimate Alexei's head spun. He bit into the red fruit, letting out a soft moan as fresh flavors hit his taste buds. Lyetah chuckled, squeezing the remaining berry against Alexei's skin and wrapping Alexei in a warm embrace. Sweet juice dropped onto Alexei's cheeks, making a sticky and delicious line from Alexei's lips to his neck.

Lyetah lapped at the red liquid, nipping Alexei's neck as he went. Alexei clung to Lyetah, holding on to the other man's clothing for dear life. The tiny bites of naughty pain sent shocks of pleasure through him. He couldn't help but push closer to Lyetah and rub against the other man. Feeling Lyetah's hard-on against his own nearly drove him out of his mind with lust.

And then, Lyetah abandoned his game and, at last, took his kiss. It wasn't relentless like Zimah's or gentle like Visnah's. Instead, it exploded over Alexei like a burst of fire, familiar, yet not, calling out the blaze Alexei always felt inside him. He seemed engulfed in liquid heat, melting, falling, losing all sense of space and humanity into this one kiss. Lyetah's tongue danced with his, and energy crackled between them, hot and intense.

When they broke apart, Alexei truly did stumble, and his clumsiness made him fall back, startling his horse. Visnah calmed the animal down with a few light pats. "Careful now. We really do want to send you home in one piece."

"And I still don't have my kiss," Ohsyn pointed out. He took Alexei's hand and pressed a light peck to his knuckles.

Visnah hugged Alexei, and Alexei accepted the embrace without question. "Go on," the other man said. "You're tired."

Zimah caressed Alexei's nape, the touch light and cool, sending shivers of pleasure through Alexei. "We won't keep you further."

Alexei wanted to be kept. In fact, as delicious as the berries looked, he wanted to return them. It seemed wrong somehow to exchange these kisses for material goods. He felt as if he were losing something special in doing so, perhaps a piece of his own soul.

"Don't be saddened," Ohsyn said. "I'm sure we'll see each other soon."

Lyetah grinned. "If nothing else, your sister is bound to have some other unreasonable demand."

"Come to us directly, *radost moia*," Visnah finished. "There's no point in exhausting yourself with a useless trip to the market."

Alexei gaped at Visnah, focusing on Visnah's piece of advice and not on the endearment. "How did you know about that?" He shook his head, guessing the men would give him another enigmatic reply. "No, never mind. It doesn't matter. Thank you."

Once again, Alexei rode off. He tried to stop himself from looking behind, but didn't manage to win the battle. Unsurprisingly, the men had vanished and all that remained were the four standing stones.

Sighing to himself, Alexei directed his horse home. What was this sudden heaviness in his heart? Could he be falling for these four men? No. He couldn't think such a thing. He knew nothing about them. They acted like the seasons incarnate and their peculiar powers should make Alexei run for the hills screaming. He had no business getting emotional over inhuman folk. As if that weren't enough, they were all male. And loving four people at the same time couldn't be, especially not after two days of knowing them.

Lost in his thoughts, he made his way home. He didn't even feel the chill, too busy musing over his erratic emotions. Once he reached their house, he led his horse into the stable then went inside. Eva met him in the hallway and gave him an expectant look. "Well? Did you get them?"

Alexei's fatigue prevented him from even replying. He didn't have the energy to focus on her nonsense. He just handed her the bag with the berries and went past her. He aimed to head straight for his room, crash into his bed, and think about his men. Unsurprisingly, Eva stopped him. "You're so rude, Alexei," she said, blocking his path. She squinted at him. "Oh, and your lips are swollen again. And why is your neck like that?"

Alexei cursed to himself. Lyetah must have left marks when he'd bit him. Just great. He did his best to look calm. "Must be bug bites," he said.

Their father came into the hallway before Eva could say anything else. "Alexei, you're back. Excellent."

"He got me strawberries, Papa," Eva piped in. "I told you he could do it."

She sounded like she'd been the one to do all the effort, but Alexei ignored her. The burning fire echoed his thoughts. *"Your sister is a fool,"* it said.

Almost chuckling at his own fancies, Alexei turned toward his father. "Sorry for taking so long," he said.

Igor's large hand landed on Alexei's shoulder. "Don't be silly, boy. Run along and get changed now. Dinner will be ready soon."

As he headed out, Alexei ran straight into Elga. She gave him a cool look but didn't say anything. When Alexei reached his room, his mind oscillated between two questions. When had his mother become a stranger? What was he going to do about his four dream lovers?

Chapter 3

The next day brought with it yet another request from Eva. As soon as Alexei entered the kitchen in hope of getting breakfast, she pounced on him. "The strawberries spoiled overnight," she cried. "I didn't even manage to eat too many."

Alexei mentally groaned. "So now I have to go get more?" he asked, exasperated. This game of Eva's started to wear on him.

To Alexei's surprise, Eva shook her head. "No. I'm sick of strawberries," she said, contradicting her own apparent dismay. "But I'd love some apples. Would you be a dear and fetch me some?"

Apples? Now she wanted apples? Alexei wanted to shake the stupidity out of her. "Fine," he said, "but this is the last thing I'm getting for you."

It made him uncomfortable to ask for things from the four men over and over. Strangely, he felt that by doing so, he disappointed them. He didn't know why or how, but they'd treated him with such affection and generosity. They'd saved his life and granted him marvelous gifts. They'd shown him magic and passion. How could he continue to take advantage of their good will? As much as they claimed a few kisses were enough as payment, Alexei didn't think it would ever be true.

Elga didn't look surprised when, at breakfast, Eva bragged about the promise she'd extracted from Alexei. She did, however, frown when Eva complained about Alexei's threat. "I don't see why you would refuse your sister. It's clearly no hardship for you to go and get the things she requires."

"I'm sorry, Mama, but I can't agree with you," he replied. "This is the last time I'm going there, and I won't be swayed."

Elga's eyes widened. Alexei had never talked back to her, but he'd never felt so strongly about something either. She looked like she wanted to say something, but Igor stopped her. "Good for you, son. I truly don't want you scampering around the forest for flowers and whatnot."

Eva's eyes shone with unshed tears, but this time, she didn't cry like before. Alexei guessed she thought she could change his mind eventually, manipulate him into complying like she always did. Alexei let her believe what he wanted. He'd made his decision.

After breakfast, Alexei took the road to the forest once again. He almost feared to see the four men again. Three times, Eva had asked him for something absurd, and three times, Alexei had appealed to them for help. There were so many things Alexei wanted to ask them, and yet, he always ended up demanding items instead.

The horse unerringly led him to the forest, and this time found the grove with reasonable ease. When they reached the familiar spot, the men once more appeared out of the blue. "Well, well," Lyetah said. "If it isn't our dear Alexei. What does your sister want now?"

Alexei couldn't look at him. "Apples," he murmured. He dismounted, keeping his eyes on the ground at all times.

Silence fell over the grove at his less than enthusiastic answer. Alexei felt Lyetah approach, and then the blond placed a finger under Alexei's chin, gently forcing their gazes to meet. "What is it, *solnyshko moyo*? Why do you look so down?"

"I don't know," Alexei murmured. "No, that's not right. I do know. It's just not right to just come here and take advantage of your kindness like this."

Lyetah smirked at him. "It's not like we don't get anything out of it."

Alexei broke away from Lyetah, disheartened. He couldn't expect them to understand. He didn't understand it himself.

Ohsyn wrapped his arms around him, and his warmth cast away some of the shadows in Alexei's mind. "It's all right, Alexei. If our little exchanges bother you, we don't have to do it."

Zimah nodded. Silently, he once again made the snow vanish. Ohsyn briefly stepped away from Alexei and made an elaborate gesture in the air and toward the ground. The trees flourished once again, the branches heavy and laden with fruit. "There you go. Take as many as you want. We don't want you upset."

Alexei stared at the apple trees, then at Ohsyn's earnest face. "I don't want to take them," he replied. "I just…"

He didn't know how to explain himself. He felt so confused and out of his depth. He shouldn't be feeling such things in the first place, especially not for men so out of his reach.

"Oh, Alexei," Visnah continued in a soft voice. "Don't be afraid. I promise you all will be well."

Visnah's soothing voice acted like a balm on Alexei's soul. When Ohsyn swooped in to steal a kiss, Alexei melted, all doubts vanishing in an instant. Ohsyn smelled intoxicating, and his taste reminded Alexei of well-aged wine. He took and gave in equal measure, generous, yet demanding, decadent, yet kind. Their bodies molded against each other perfectly, and for a little while, Alexei just lost himself in the dance of their tongues, in the rocking of their bodies and the musk of male arousal.

When they broke apart, Ohsyn grinned at Alexei. "There you go—my reward for the apples," he said. Alexei almost thought Ohsyn had missed the point entirely, but then the other man pressed his lips to Alexei's once again. This time, when the kiss ended, Ohsyn murmured, "And this one is because I want to, because you want to."

It was a statement, but Alexei felt the question behind it. He nodded, his face hot with desire and embarrassment.

"Now that this little problem is settled, come here and sit by our side."

Alexei allowed Lyetah to lead him next to the four large stones. Uncertain anticipation coursed through him. Lyetah knelt in the soft grass and pulled Alexei down. Their bodies collided and sparks flew between them, just like the day before.

As if of their own accord, Alexei's hands slipped between their bodies to unbutton Lyetah's shirt. Alexei idly noted the yellow material matched Lyetah's hair and tried to focus on the bland fact to give himself the courage to finish his self-appointed task. He failed, nervousness making his body tremble and his heart thunder. "Don't worry, *solnyshko moyo*," Lyetah said soothingly. "I'll take care of it."

And so, Lyetah did. Under Alexei's amazed eyes, the shirt melted, as did the bright red breeches. Alexei found himself seated in the lap of a very naked Lyetah. He froze, not knowing what to do. Sure, he'd dreamed about touching and being touched by these men, but acting out his fantasies was a different matter entirely.

"Relax, *miliy moi*," Ohsyn whispered in his ear, startling him. Ohsyn sat next to them, facing Alexei. "This is all about what we all want, remember?"

Yes, Alexei remembered. In a sense, it had been his idea to begin with. He'd wanted their kisses to be genuine—not that he considered the ones before false, but this felt different somehow.

"Just enjoy," Visnah said behind him. Alexei turned, only to watch Visnah and Zimah approach as well.

He didn't know what to say, how to act. This entire thing felt surreal, as if it couldn't possibly be happening to him. He was just Alexei. Four hot men couldn't want him, shouldn't want him.

"Don't worry," Lyetah answered. "We won't do anything you're uncomfortable with."

Lyetah had summoned his clothing back and even if Alexei could still feel the man's hard-on beneath him, he almost wept at his own stupidity.

"How about we just take things slow?" Visnah suggested.

Lyetah nodded toward Visnah and placed Alexei on the grass. "Lay down, *solnyshko moyo*," he whispered. "We'll take care of you."

Alexei obeyed. The grass felt soft, welcoming him in its green embrace. Above him, the tree branches laden with fruit sent tantalizing aromas toward him. Alexei closed his eyes. So many scents surrounded him—apples, wine, fresh flowers, and even the scent of sunlight and snow. He didn't know how he could differentiate each and every one, but he did.

Warm lips landed on his own, gentle and comforting. Visnah caressed his hair, murmuring endearments between kisses. Meanwhile, strong hands worked at his breeches. When a fist enclosed Alexei's shaft in a tight hold, Alexei tensed and opened his eyes.

Zimah's heavy hand held him down. "Don't worry. You're safe with us."

The white-haired man took position to Alexei's left, slowly unbuttoning his shirt. His cool hands sent pleasant goose bumps over Alexei's skin. While Zimah explored Alexei's torso, Ohsyn and Lyetah took off his boots and pants. Before he knew it, he ended up nearly bare under the eyes of the four men.

It was strangely arousing to be naked when all of them still wore their clothes. Still, Alexei felt a bit self-conscious. He'd never actually shown his body to anyone, not since he'd grown into an adult, at least. A lingering pang of inadequacy prodded at his mind. What if they didn't like the way he looked?

"Alexei?" Visnah said. "Everything all right? Are we going too fast? Zimah, let him go."

Zimah began to move away, but Alexei caught him. He didn't want to lose contact with any of his men. It suddenly seemed as if this moment defined his very life, as if he'd been born to be theirs. At least once, he'd allow himself to experience their passion without doubting or fearing. He'd worry about the outcome later.

"No," he said. "I want this. I want you."

He met Zimah's eyes, and in those unfathomable blue depths, he saw a deep blaze emerge. Somehow, he knew it was the flame of his own heart. He didn't have time to contemplate this because Zimah took Visnah's place. He ravished Alexei's mouth with his own. Impossibly, the kiss seemed even more intense than the day before.

Visnah's mouth enclosed around Alexei's right nipple, lapping and nipping at the small bud. The teasing sensations molded with Zimah's sensual assault, the energies of winter and spring flowing over him at the same time.

Wet heat surrounded his cock as Lyetah began sucking his dick in earnest. Alexei had fantasized about this exact thing just a few days back, but his daydream paled in comparison with reality. Just when he thought it couldn't get any better, Ohsyn's hands began to caress Alexei's legs. Ohsyn's tongue explored Alexei's thighs and up to his knees, even going down to suck on his toes. Alexei never realized those areas of his body could be so sensitive, but Ohsyn's every touch seemed to awaken nerves he hadn't even known existed.

It seemed to Alexei no inch of him went unexplored. His cock throbbed in Lyetah's mouth, demanding release, the heat the other man radiated pooling into his testes. At the same time, Zimah's kiss told him to be patient, to make things last, to take his pleasure without rushing. Wordlessly, Zimah disciplined him when Alexei would have just burst forward, too greedy for their touch to even consider waiting. The kisses they shared tempered him, and yet, fueled the blaze swallowing Alexei whole.

Visnah alternated between gentle laps and teasing bites, just like spring occasionally reverted to colder, harsher weather. In spite of the delicious ecstasy, Alexei found their measured strokes kept him close to coming, without allowing him to do so.

But Alexei allowed himself to enjoy it, to take everything they offered and revel in it. He should have been ashamed of himself for accepting their caresses, but right now, he didn't give a damn.

Still, he realized he could not hold still and, on instinct, tried to push up into Lyetah's mouth. Lyetah chuckled, and the vibrations traveled straight through Alexei's dick, making him gasp in pleasure. At the same time, his lover held him down, the pressure on his hips combining with the perfect suction in a unique blend. Ohsyn's caresses became even bolder, and his tongue left trails of fire all over Alexei's skin. Oh, it was so good, so perfect, and Alexei needed to come so badly he would have begged for it.

The ecstasy escalated to unbearable proportions, the onslaught of the four men on his body too intense for him to bear. He cried out in Zimah's mouth, his climax sweeping through him, turning him into a creature of sheer sensation. Only he and his men remained. The rest of the world dissipated, unimportant, abandoned.

He didn't know how long he floated in the orgasmic daze, but when he recovered, the first thing he saw was Zimah's beautiful eyes. And quite a sight they were, like one of the rare warm winter mornings when the promise of spring loomed ahead and the sun shone over the beautiful snowy hills.

"Hello there," Zimah said. "You okay?"

"Never better," Alexei replied breathlessly. When his mind began to work, he realized they'd all focused on him, and he'd just selfishly taken without giving anything back, again. "What about you?" he said, his gaze going from Zimah to Visnah, Lyetah, and Ohsyn.

"Don't worry about us," Ohsyn replied, smiling. "We're fine. We have time to explore all possibilities."

Visnah nodded. "Better not to rush."

Alexei began to protest. "But…"

Lyetah pressed a finger to his lips. "Trust us, all right?" He began to help Alexei into his clothing. Alexei helped insofar as he could, still troubled by their refusal.

"Seriously, *lyubimiy moi*, don't look so glum," Zimah said. "It's not like we're all alone and abandoned here."

A wink from Lyetah made Alexei grasp the meaning of Zimah's words. The four of them were lovers. It made sense, in a way. Just like the seasons fit together, so did these men. But Alexei didn't know what to think about that. He didn't want to interfere in their relationship or spoil what they had.

"You're thinking too hard again," Visnah whispered. "Don't doubt what you know to be true."

Alexei nodded. He clung to Visnah's reassuring words, forcing himself to stop dwelling over glum predictions. "And on that note, Alexei, you need to pick your apples," Ohsyn said.

Alexei gasped as he realized the reason why he'd been sent here in the first place. He'd forgotten about Eva and her fruit entirely. Sure, his family didn't know how long the trip to the grove took. Alexei could spend some more time here with his men. "I don't want to go," he said. "I just want to be here with you."

"I know," Lyetah answered. "That time will come. You have to be patient."

Sighing, Alexei picked a couple of apples and placed them in his saddlebag. Afterwards, he turned to his men. "When will I see you again?"

"Soon," Visnah answered. "For now, go on home. And remember, we'll miss you."

On impulse, Alexei stole another kiss from each of his men. He hated saying goodbye, especially now, when it meant being separated from his lovers. But he forced himself to be strong and break away from them. "I'll miss you, too."

He got on his horse and rode off. Behind him, he felt a slight whisper of the wind and knew his men had vanished. His mind and heart in turmoil, he headed home.

Predictably, upon his arrival, Eva snatched the apples without even a thank you. Yet again, she commented on his swollen lips, and he ignored her. Huffing, Eva took her apples to her room while Alexei sat in front of the crackling fire. What would happen tomorrow?

Would he really see his lovers again, or had it all been a weird hallucination? What were these newly emerging feelings in his heart? So many questions, so few answers. For once, the fire didn't speak to him, leaving Alexei alone and lost in his dilemmas.

Chapter 4

The following day had Alexei still dwelling on the memories of the incredible orgasm he'd experienced at the four men's hands and clever mouths. He'd slept poorly, tormented by sensual dreams, and now, his mind kept drifting off to ice-blue or amber eyes, gentle voices, and sweet, wine-tasting lips.

Even Igor noticed the change in him. Concerned, he urged Alexei to get some rest. "You've run around too much these days. Perhaps you're coming down with something." Alexei's father shook his head. "I knew I shouldn't have allowed you to leave in such weather."

Alexei accepted his father's kindness shamelessly. He knew that if he tried to get some work done today, he'd just be in the way. He simply couldn't focus on chores when his entire being ached to just feel his men close. Even hearing their voices would have sufficed.

Sitting by the fire helped, however, the flame singing a low chant to him. *"You'll be with them,"* it said. *"Don't fret and be patient."*

Unfortunately, Eva intruded on his moment of peace and quiet. "Alexei? Oh, Alexei, would you come over here for a moment?"

Alexei gave his sister a bored look. "You come if you want to."

He knew she would not do it. Eva never sat down in front of the fire. In fact, excessive heat made her violently ill.

Eva frowned at him. "Stop being such a jerk. I asked you nicely."

"If you want something, just say it from there," he said. Whatever urged her to approach him couldn't be good, Alexei just knew it.

Eva crossed her hands over her chest and huffed. "Fine. Since you're clearly not busy today, I want you to go get me more apples. The ones you brought yesterday dried up already."

Alexei couldn't bring himself to be surprised by her request. She seemed to be getting more and more spoiled by the second, and indulging her whims didn't help. "Like I said yesterday," he answered, "I'm not doing it again."

"Right," Eva drawled, "you're afraid of a little winter wind. Poor little Alexei." She laughed, and Alexei forced himself to remain calm.

"And how many times did you leave the house last summer, hmm?" he asked. "At least I don't hide in my room like you."

Unfortunately, Elga chose this particular moment to come inside. "Don't talk to your sister like that," she said. "If she wants apples, you'll get her apples."

Alexei shot to his feet. "I said no more after yesterday, and I haven't changed my mind."

Eva let out a sigh of theatrical exasperation. "Fine. Then can you just show me the way? From now on, I'll get my own fruit."

Alexei's mind went blank. He started to come up with an argument, but knew he'd been defeated. "You can't be serious," he tried to say. "What's the point of going trekking through the forest? You ate apples yesterday. Just drop it."

"I don't want to," Eva answered stubbornly. "And if you won't do it, I will."

Elga looked like she doubted the success of this plan. "Darling, I don't know if it's wise. The road is too long and dangerous."

Pain coursed through Alexei at the sight of their mother fussing over Eva so visibly. She hadn't shown a trickle of concern for him. Granted, Alexei was male and could take care of himself better, but she knew his vulnerability to the cold. She could have at least acknowledged it.

"Mama is right, Eva. It is too risky for you," he said tiredly.

"No, it's not." His sister shook her head. "I'll be just fine. You just need to show me the way, and I'll stop bothering you."

A few hours later, Alexei and Eva left their house on his horse. Alexei still couldn't figure out how she'd managed to convince them all, their parents included. But he felt terrified she would discover the truth about his four lovers. What would she do if she saw them? Would they ask her for kisses, just like they had with him? Jealousy and fear swelled inside him, terrible and hurtful. For the first time, he hoped his men would not make their appearance, or he would not manage to find the grove.

Halfway to their destination, Eva complained she could no longer withstand riding. She was not used to it, so Alexei didn't hold it against her. However, he couldn't refrain from pointing out that she should have expected such difficulties. "How easy did you think it would be?" he asked as he helped her dismount.

She frowned at him. "It's just an animal. I didn't think mounting it would actually hurt me. Let's just walk for a while."

Of course, Eva's proposed method ended up taking more out of Alexei than out of her. As the cold wind intensified, Eva seemed to gain more and more strength, and Alexei weakened. After a while, Alexei suggested riding the horse again, arguing that it would be faster, but Eva declined. "What point is there to be fast if I'm going to be in pain? Come on, lazy bones. Move it."

And so, Alexei resigned himself to accepting the cold trek. In the end, walking didn't prove to be quite so bad, since the effort heated Alexei up. Eva soon seemed to show signs of fatigue, and Alexei guessed it must be happening to her as well.

The trip seemed to take forever. Several times, Alexei considered just forcing Eva onto the horse and heading back home, but something stopped him. The blaze inside him rebelled at the thought of giving up in front of a challenge. So onward they went until they at last spotted the woods in the distance.

They stopped to catch their breath at the very edge of the forest. "Here we are," Alexei said, "but there's still quite a way to go to reach the grove."

Eva nodded, scanning the area thoughtfully. "The shrubbery seems very thick."

"I suppose," Alexei answered, not really understanding what she meant to say by that.

"It's going to be difficult to move with this big, useless beast behind us," she said. Before Alexei could stop her, she stole the reins of the horse from him and kicked the poor animal hard. The horse neighed in protest and took off in a heavy gallop.

Alexei rushed after the animal and called out, but, predictably, it ignored him. Furious, he stalked back to his sister. "Are you mad? How are we going to get home?"

Eva arched a brow at him. "Walking, of course, just like we came."

"You idiot!" Alexei shouted. "Can't you see it will be getting dark soon? When night falls, the woods will be teeming with wolves and the road with bandits. And what about your many apples? How do you intend to carry them?"

Eva's eyes widened. Obviously, she hadn't considered those aspects. She'd always disliked animals since she considered them dirty and disgusting. It was just like her to disregard their safety for something so trivial.

In that moment, she looked so very young Alexei didn't have the heart to continue a shouting match. "Look, let's just head on home, and we should be fine. If we keep a good pace, we'll reach the house before dusk."

To his surprise and dismay, Eva shook her head. "No. We've come this far already. We're not going back."

"Eva, be reasonable," he started to say.

He shouldn't have bothered with trying to convince her. She took off, running straight into the forest. Alexei cursed and rushed after her. The foolish girl would get herself killed. Even if the cold didn't hurt her, the wolves certainly would.

Desperate, he tried to find his sister, calling out her name. On and on he searched, acutely aware of every second that passed. Even if they didn't get along, Eva was his twin and he loved her. In his heart, he'd always hoped they'd get over their differences one day. They wouldn't have this chance if something happened to Eva.

He tried to follow the footsteps in the snow, but Eva moved on light feet, barely leaving any trace at all. Darkness began to creep into the forest, ominous and threatening. A feeling of decision invaded him, a hidden warmth fueling his body from deep inside. He would not allow any harm to come to his sister.

As his mind cleared, he could sense the way she'd gone. He rushed in that direction when, out of the blue, a bloodcurdling scream sounded straight ahead. "Alexei!"

It was Eva's voice, and the terror in it turned Alexei's blood into ice. He moved as quickly as he could, and at last, saw his sister ahead. She lay still on the ground, her eyes fixed somewhere in front of her.

Alexei reached her side and realized why she'd screamed. In the pale light of dusk, he spotted the wolves approach. Oh, Goddess. This couldn't be happening.

Trying to keep his composure, he knelt at Eva's side. "Are you all right, Eva?"

"I tripped against a root," Eva whispered back. She showed him her bloody hand. "I scratched myself when I fell."

The wolves must have scented Eva's blood in the air then and come hunting before they usually did. "Can you walk?" he asked. The beasts were approaching now, and it would only be a matter of seconds for them to attack.

She nodded. "I can walk. I didn't twist my ankle."

Alexei gently helped her up, careful so as not to make any sudden movements. "When I say go, run back as fast as you can. Try to find your way to the road using my footsteps."

"But Alexei…" she protested. Her eyes filled with tears, and for once, they looked genuine.

"Shh, *sestrichka*," Alexei murmured. "It will be fine."

They'd never used terms of endearment with each other, not even as children, but somehow, in this moment, it fit. Eva seemed to think the same. "*Bratishka*," she murmured, "I don't want to leave you."

Eva's words meant the world to Alexei, but he couldn't allow her to stay. "You have to go. Our parents are going to need you."

They didn't have time to continue the debate. The wolves lunged, their wild eyes shining with hunger. Alexei pushed Eva onto the path and positioned himself strategically between her way out and the wolves. One of the animals pounced on Alexei, embedding its fangs in his flesh and sending him crashing into the cool ground. Alexei knew he was going to die here. He wished he could have seen his men one last time. But at least his sister would escape.

Unfortunately, the wolves were more numerous than Alexei had originally thought. He heard Eva scream and realized they'd been surrounded by a whole pack of the beasts.

He didn't know how it happened, but upon his sister's desperate shout, he felt a deep blaze swell inside him, the same thing that always kept him from abandoning a job he disliked. Fire burst out of his very heart, and the wolf that had attacked him went flying into the air with a pained yelp.

Dazed, Alexei struggled to his feet and looked around, searching for Eva. He found her just a few feet away from him, staring at a snow drift that hadn't been there before. Wolves attempted to get out of the icy trap. It seemed like an odd dream, and Alexei expected to wake any moment now.

He tried to push the wolves back using the fire he could suddenly summon, but he the heat inside him soon began to get unbearable. Alexei had never been hurt by warmth before, but this fever sent agony into his brain. He threw his gaze back toward his sister, and saw her lips had gone blue and her body very still. They would not be able to hang on for much longer.

Just when he thought all was lost, he felt a familiar presence close in. It brought with it a soothing touch, and in spite of the molten heat torturing him, his mind and vision cleared up a bit. His men surrounded him and Eva, their power so palpable that it made Alexei both humbled and awed.

A slideshow of images flashed around him. The ground seemed to shift from winter, to spring, summer and autumn, rain, hail, and light all flaring around them. When it was over, the wolves had vanished, gone to hide from the more powerful opponent.

Overwhelming relief filled Alexei, bringing with it a striking feeling of exhaustion. He could not have held himself upright to save his life. His knees buckled, and he swooned, threatening to fall to the ground once again. Visnah caught him and pulled him against his solid warmth. "Oh, *radost moia*, we're so sorry," Visnah whispered. "We should have gotten here sooner."

"This should have never happened," Ohsyn said, his voice laced with pain.

Alexei clung to his lovers, finding comfort in their presence. He wanted to tell them it was all right, that he didn't blame them for not being here, but his concern for Eva won over his desire to soothe them. "Eva?" he asked.

"She will be fine." Zimah's voice held strength and decision. "You will both be fine." His tone turned a touch rougher when he spoke again, this time to his three companions. "Come on. We need to hurry."

Zimah took Alexei from Visnah, lifting him in his arms while Lyetah carried Eva. Zimah's cool body sent away some of the painful heat, but Alexei felt tired, so very tired. "Don't fall asleep, *lyubimiy moi*," Zimah said. "Stay with me. Hang in there, just a little longer."

It suddenly seemed very important for Alexei to tell them how he felt. "Thank you," he whispered, hoping all of them would hear. "Thank you for showing me passion and… and making me feel these incredible things. I wish… I wish we could have more time together. Please, help Eva, and remember me fondly."

Chapter 5

Alexei was dying. Zimah knew it, as did all the others. He could see it in the way Alexei's bright red hair clung limply to his sweaty forehead. His beautiful coal-black eyes shut when he surrendered to unconsciousness. Eva seemed in a similar state, and Zimah knew it all amounted to the foolishness and disregard the four of them had shown.

He still remembered the day when Alexei and Eva had been conceived. As earth spirits, Zimah and his lovers were assigned to watch over the land in their particular assigned territory. Sometimes, however, they fulfilled wishes, and when they'd seen the middle-aged woman happily dancing in the snow and making a snow angel, they'd decided of common accord to give the couple the child they desired so much.

* * * *

Twenty five years ago

"Poor humans," Visnah said. "They desire a baby so much, and they just haven't been granted one."

"Perhaps we can help," Ohsyn suggested.

Zimah nodded. "Together, we can make the snow angel flesh. Should the Goddess will it so, She will send Her power to grant it life and soul."

They waited until the couple returned to their home. The four men got out of their hiding place. Humans couldn't actually see them, but they didn't want to risk performing magic with them present. Zimah lifted his hands in the air and blew over the snow. The snow angel began to take shape, its form floating from the ground to create an ethereal silhouette in the air. The beautiful face of a young girl shone in Zimah's vision, not yet a physical form, but there, just within his reach.

"She needs something more," Visnah said.

Lyetah spoke for the first time. "Fire. She needs fire."

Zimah hated to agree with his sun-dedicated lover. The two of them always struggled to balance their relationship since Lyetah insisted on the importance of a fiery heart, while Zimah believed a cool head meant the most for a successful individual. Secretly, however, he acknowledged Lyetah might be right. Humans could not live with cold hearts. No one could, not even earth spirits. Zimah himself had been cold and indifferent once, but his lovers balanced him, giving him emotion. This girl needed something similar. She needed a spark of flame to grant her a kind heart.

So he nodded while Lyetah threw a gaze toward the burning fire inside the Igor and Elga's home. "We'll use that," Lyetah said.

He murmured a small chant under his breath, and sparks of embers began to float from the fire. They swirled into the air, naughty, playful, and daring. Zimah took Lyetah's hand and, together with Ohsyn and Visnah, they began to unite the snow angel with the sparks. The figure of the snow angel floated inside. It headed toward the sleeping Elga, the sparks close behind it. At the same time, the two fell upon Elga's body, granting her fertility.

That night, when Igor consummated his union with Elga, the magic Zimah and his lovers used took root. Nine months afterwards, they found out Elga bore twins, one created out of flame, the other out of snow.

* * * *

The memories flashed through his mind as Zimah ran. They should have been more careful. They'd realized the chill in Eva's heart spread over Elga and had been helpless to stop it. Alexei's fire helped Igor, but the four of them had known they needed to intervene before it was too late. And so, when Eva began with her unreasonable requests, they'd found the right moment to approach Alexei. They'd hoped to become Alexei's support and, eventually, find a way for his sister to reach her true potential. Zimah never expected to fall for the young man in the process.

Unfortunately, their incipient plan had caused a disaster, setting in motion the events that caused Alexei's doom. Unfortunately, not even earth spirits could be omnipresent and omniscient. They'd felt Alexei approach, of course, but had not realized the situation could end up like this. In the past, Alexei never experienced any trouble in getting through the forest, but Eva's presence and clumsiness caused the two to get attacked by wolves. As soon as Zimah and the others sensed Alexei's distress, they'd come to look for the twins, but they hadn't reached them in time.

Alexei's injury from the wolf bite could have been healed, but the worst of the damage didn't come from the animals. The spark of magic inside Alexei and Eva had emerged when they'd seen one another in peril. The twin bond made their powers blast through, pushing back the outside opponent. However, mortal bodies were not made to contain such magic. In spite of Alexei and Eva's resilience to their particular element, the twins were, in the end, humans, and their inner organs could not withstand extreme temperatures. Zimah did his best to chill Alexei down, but he knew at this point, the situation was beyond them.

And so, they took the two humans deep into the forest, each passing moment sealing the twins' fate. At last, the standing stones were in sight. A portal to the spirit world and their home lay beyond, the one place where they could prevent Alexei and Eva from slipping away before Zimah and his lovers could find a solution.

No one else could use the portal but them, and they passed through the magical field, emerging at the other side. Their house held the character of each of them, both cool and warm, a fact for which Zimah felt very grateful now.

In the main room, a tamed fire offered enough warmth for it to be comfortable for all. Zimah's room was, predictably, the chilliest, but Visnah's maintained a pleasant temperature, a refreshing spring breeze blowing through windows made out sheer ivy. They placed both Eva and Alexei there, judging the moderate temperature would be best for them. Being close to each other would help them as well, through their bond of twins. But the two couldn't be kept here for much longer, or their bodies would fade away into nothingness.

Turning toward his lovers, Zimah asked, "What do we do now?"

* * * *

For the first time in memory, Zimah looked lost. It struck Visnah with the intensity of a lightning bolt. Zimah had always been the cool-headed one out of all of them. His outbursts of temper, mostly caused by a conflict between him and Lyetah, were always as terrible as winter storms, but Visnah and Ohsyn managed to calm him down without fail.

And yet, in spite of all the time they'd spent together, Visnah had never actually seen Zimah afraid, not knowing what to do.

Visnah didn't blame him. Alexei effectively swept them all off their feet. They'd watched over him from afar, and to a certain extent, admired him once he grew up into a man. But never once had it occurred to them that they would fall so hard for the human born out of a flame in the hearth. Visnah himself couldn't believe it. Alexei melted Zimah's cold demeanor, accepted Lyetah's unrestrained passion with no qualms, and took in Visnah's gentle nature and Ohsyn's generosity without taking advantage of them. Strong, handsome, and with a kind and loving heart, Alexei filled a gap in their life they'd never wanted to acknowledge, strengthening their bond.

But Alexei and his sister, Eva, were now on the brink of death in Visnah's own room. Visnah could only think of one solution for their predicament. Earth spirits didn't typically ask for things from the Goddess. They'd been already gifted with so much—love, power, eternal youth—that they couldn't in good conscience make other demands. Their prayers mostly held the welfare of others and thanks for what they'd been given.

But now, for the first time, Visnah would ask something for himself. With a thought, Visnah left the room and manifested into their holy garden. Their world was not like the mortal realm. Here, time had no meaning, and space could be molded according to their desires. One single spot remained unchanging, no matter what—the shrine dedicated to the omnipotent Goddess.

He sensed his lovers appear behind him, and, together, they knelt in the grass. Threads of gold wove from the simple altar, then down toward the ground, molding with the very fabric of their existence. Visnah closed his eyes and prayed. "Please, Goddess, give us advice. Tell us how to save them."

His lovers' voices joined him in a low murmur, in patterns of worshipping psalms that sounded almost hypnotic. He didn't know how long they just knelt there. It could have been a moment or an age. Visnah felt the touch inside him, and an image filled his mind. Fire and ice, death for life.

Visnah's eyes shot open, and he looked back toward his lovers. Judging by their expressions of horror, they'd seen the same thing. Not even Zimah could mask his dismay, and Lyetah looked very pale. Ohsyn clutched the grass with such strength that it withered under his touch.

Visnah knew exactly what they felt. For the first time in his entire existence, he doubted the advice of the Goddess. How could this be?

He struggled to his feet, the shock too powerful for him to contain. To his surprise, a tear streamed down his cheek, falling to the ground and promptly turning into a pale snowdrop. He hastily wiped his eyes and took a deep breath. He couldn't falter now. He needed to be strong for all of them. "Come on," he told his lovers. "Let's go back inside."

They nodded and, together, faded once more through the ethereal. In Visnah's room, they knelt next to the bed where Alexei and Eva lay. Predictably, they looked worse. Frost now covered Eva's side of the bed, while Alexei's seemed scorched. Alexei's hair almost looked like it had turned to liquid flame, the red color even more intense than before.

"There's nothing we can do, is there?" Ohsyn said. "There really is no other way."

Visnah nodded, even as pain coursed through him. "We just have to trust and hope."

Visnah pressed his palm to Alexei's and hissed when their skin made contact. He found himself forced to pull his burnt hand back. No wonder the sheets were in this state. Alexei's temperature had risen greatly. If he'd been in the mortal realm, his brain would have shut down by now.

Zimah glanced at Visnah's palm and took it in his own. Few things could hurt an earth spirit, but apparently, spiritual fire had that ability. Visnah allowed his energy to mold with Zimah's and felt his burn heal. As they finished, he saw Lyetah and Ohsyn had grabbed the twins, paying extra care not to touch their skin.

They rushed out of Visnah's room and headed out. Lyetah hesitated upon reaching the exit, and the barrier between worlds. "Perhaps it would be best if you and Ohsyn stayed here with them, while Zimah and I go make the preparations into the mortal world. We don't know how long they are going to last there."

Visnah nodded and took Alexei from Lyetah. It hurt to know that he couldn't touch Alexei without being burnt, but it hurt even more to acknowledge what they were going to do. As Zimah and Lyetah left through the portal, Visnah held Alexei as close as he could and prayed once more.

* * * *

Lyetah exited the portal between the realms, closely followed by Zimah. He knew they didn't have much time before Alexei and Eva's bodies yielded the battle. The thought gave him focus when all he wanted to do was scream at the injustice. In moments such as these, he understood the doubts humans always went through regarding the existence of divinity.

He acknowledged his own blasphemy, but he couldn't help it. It just seemed too cruel. But Lyetah needed to cling to his faith and hope for the best. The Goddess always took care of them. She would not abandon them now.

Unfortunately, due to the nature of their task, he ended up the one assigned to deal with Alexei's part of the vision. He waited while Zimah dissipated the snow, then proceeded to gather sticks of wood from the forest. They worked in silence, and Lyetah forced himself not to think of the purpose of what he meant to construct.

At last, he acquired enough materials and started to build. When he finished, a strong pyre rose in the middle of the grove with plenty of wood to fuel the fire. Lyetah threw a glance Zimah's way and saw his wintry lover had finished as well. Zimah's glum task had been to prepare a coffin made out of sheer ice.

"Start the fire," Zimah said, his voice level. "I'll go and get the others."

As Zimah disappeared beyond the standing stones, Lyetah summoned the heat intrinsic to his element and directed it toward the wood. Fire soon engulfed the base of the pyre, and not a moment too soon. His three lovers emerged once more, the twins in their grasp.

They stared at each other, then at the coffin and the pyre. Visnah's green eyes turned almost blue with sorrow. Lyetah made his way to Visnah's side and reached for Alexei. "Let me." He could not allow his gentle lover to do this. It would break Visnah's heart even more.

Visnah opened his mouth to say something, but before he could speak, a moan from Eva drew their attention. Perhaps the heat from the pyre caused her to stir. Oh, Goddess. How were they going to do this with them awake? "Alexei," she murmured, eyes dazed. "What is happening to me?"

Zimah took hold of the young girl. "Shh, *malen'kaya printsessa*. Don't be afraid. Everything will be all right."

He stood by the icy coffin and gave Lyetah a telling look. They had to this at the same time for it to work. And as much as they hated freezing a young girl alive, burning Alexei would be even more difficult.

Thankfully, by some divine intervention, Alexei did not regain consciousness. Lyetah snatched the youth from Visnah's arms. By now, the heat from the pyre had increased greatly, and it would have been uncomfortable for anyone else anyway. He couldn't help but touch Alexei one last time. Alexei's feverish skin even burnt him, but he held on. "Farewell, *solnyshko moyo*," he whispered.

With his heart full of sorrow, he pushed Alexei's body into the pyre. Behind him, he heard a light cry, then nothing. He turned and realized Zimah had done his part. Eva now lay beneath the heavy ice, locked inside, still beautiful, and forever cold.

The flame from the fire seemed to burn brighter and brighter. When Lyetah looked toward it once again, he caught sight of the evil flame tearing into flesh, destroying Alexei's beauty. What had he done? What had he expected? Perhaps he'd hoped an angel would emerge and stop him from committing this sin.

He could not bear it. He couldn't just stand there and watch this happen. He lunged forward, fully intending to jump into the fire after Alexei, but strong arms pulled him back, stopping him from doing so.

"Don't," Ohsyn said in his ear. "There's nothing we can do about it now, just hope and pray."

All strength went out of Lyetah. He felt as if the sun always inside him no longer shone. How could he push Alexei into the fire? Why hadn't he found another way?

He sank to his knees, his only comfort Ohsyn's embrace. "Hush," Ohsyn murmured. "It's going to be fine. You didn't do anything wrong."

Lyetah wanted to believe that, but the smell of the burning fire filled his nostrils, and he couldn't get the image of Alexei turning into a charred corpse out of his mind. He didn't think he ever would.

* * * *

Ohsyn held Lyetah close, his mind reeling with the events of the past hour. He couldn't even fathom how Lyetah felt at watching Alexei burn on the pyre. Ohsyn's own heart was breaking, and he hadn't pushed Alexei in. But Lyetah had done what none of them would've been able to do, and as crazy as it seemed, Ohsyn still kept hope.

He forced Lyetah to face away from the pyre, knowing the sight of it would just make things worse. He hugged Lyetah's trembling body and whispered into his lover's ear, "Do you remember how we met?"

Lyetah nodded and let out a low, sad chuckle. "How could I forget?"

They'd all been so young and so new at being earth spirits. Each of them had been born out of their particular element, molded into a new life form by the creator. At that time, neither of them understood how their new tasked worked. But then the Goddess united them in one team to protect these distant lands. At first, they'd barely gotten along, but soon, they'd found a balance in and through each other.

"The Goddess knew what She was doing when She gathered us together. You have to stand by your faith. She knows what She is doing now."

Ohsyn did his best to sound confident when he felt anything but. Truly, he couldn't help but doubt. He wanted to believe with a desperate intensity, but when faced with the burning fire that consumed Alexei's mortal form, it wasn't so easy.

He comforted himself with the thought that Alexei's soul remained immortal, like all souls. If they'd indeed lost Alexei, Ohsyn trusted that one day, they'd find him again in a different land and a different time. They would be given a second chance. Ohsyn couldn't even accept the alternative.

Lyetah placed his head on Ohsyn's shoulder, and Ohsyn threaded his hand through his lover's locks, gently caressing him. He knew Visnah and Zimah needed him as well, so he felt thankful when the two joined him and Lyetah, and they knelt together in the grass. They just sat there for the longest time in the middle of the ageless grove at the border between the spirit world and the mortal realm.

At last, the fire of the pyre began to dwindle, and Lyetah stirred, looking back toward the burnt wood. There was no sign of Alexei, Ohsyn realized. He didn't know if he should be happy or sad about that, but perhaps it would be for the best. He didn't think he could have withstood the sight of Alexei's dead body, and he kept his hopeful façade.

"He's gone," Lyetah murmured, his voice strangled and full of pain. "I killed him."

"You didn't kill him, Lyetah," Ohsyn insisted. "This happened because of the fire inside Alexei. It burnt him out in the end. There was nothing we could do."

"Stop saying that!" Lyetah shouted. He glowered at Ohsyn, his fury so intense it struck Ohsyn almost physically. "Stop trying to make me feel better. Show some sort of emotion!"

Ohsyn felt his own anger flare and tried to control it. They were all dual, just like the seasons whose energy they bore. In winter, beautiful snowflakes fell in a peaceful dance, but their perfection could be torn apart by the fury of the storms. Spring meant renewed life and hope, yet could bring deadly floods. In the summer, the sun shone brightly, regaling the humans with rich crops and pleasant weather. But the same rays could be destructive and cause drought and famine. And at last, autumn gifted the world with generous produce, only to take it all away when furious hail and rain fell. Similarly, Ohsyn and his lovers could protect and do harm at the same time. In this particular moment, Ohsyn's dark side was emerging.

Visnah got up and set himself between Ohsyn and Lyetah. "Calm down. Arguing won't help us."

"At least it's something," Lyetah shot back. "I can't bear listening to you, all resigned and accepting."

Ohsyn gritted his teeth at Lyetah's unreasonable accusation. "And what would you have me do? Die? Do you think Alexei would want us to do that?"

"No," a sudden voice said. "I wouldn't want it."

Ohsyn turned toward the pyre once more. The dying flames seemed to materialize into a figure until finally, they revealed Alexei's shape. He looked like an avenging angel, his entire body ablaze, yet still so very beautiful.

Alexei stepped down from the pyre, his eyes burning coals fixed on them. "Thank you for having the strength to save me. I don't think I could've done this in your place." The flames began to melt until at last, they revealed skin. "Thank you for everything," Alexei whispered.

Ohsyn lunged forward, saving Alexei from collapsing to the ground. Instinctively, he pressed his lips to Alexei's forehead, just wanting to feel the other man was there, safe. As he did so, he realized Alexei's skin temperature had normalized. Strikingly, even if he'd come out of a pyre, Alexei seemed all right.

But beneath the appearance of normality, Ohsyn did feel the change. Alexei's mortality had been traded for a higher level of existence. Ohsyn couldn't identify it, not yet, but he sent a prayer of thanks and apology to the Goddess. They never should have doubted. The Goddess wouldn't have given them Alexei if She intended to take the youth away.

Alexei gave him an exhausted look. "Please, don't fight," he said. After a short pause, he asked, "Eva?"

Ohsyn's heart fell. How would they tell Alexei they'd frozen his sister alive? He saw no easy way to do it, so he gently took Alexei in his arms and carried him there. Alexei tensed when he saw his sister inside the icy coffin. "Is she dead?" he asked, his voice trembling.

Ohsyn didn't know the answer to that question. For a few terrible minutes, he'd been convinced of Alexei's death. To his surprise, an image flashed through his mind, giving him the requested answer. A princess, trapped in a prison of ice, to be rescued by her fated soul mate.

"Her spirit is sleeping," he told Alexei. "But she can and will be awakened. We just need to find the right person to do it."

"Her true love," Lyetah explained. He seemed to have recovered from his earlier distress. Together with the others, he joined Ohsyn and Alexei next to the coffin.

In Lyetah's eyes, Ohsyn read the same desire to feel Alexei he himself had experienced. Ohsyn handed Alexei to Lyetah. "I'll make some arrangements for her to be taken care of. Worry not. All will be well."

Lyetah seated Alexei against one of the trees with Zimah and Visnah joining him. They all gave him troubled looks, obviously reluctant to let him go. Ohsyn smiled at them. "I will be back soon. *Miliy moi*, get some rest. You need it."

Alexei nodded, his eyes already closing. As the young man dozed off, Ohsyn lifted Eva's coffin in his arms. It was heavy, but Ohsyn had no real trouble carrying it. He wished he could have used magic to transport it, but alas, it was too risky with her inside.

He chose a spot at the outer edge of the grove for her resting place. There, he summoned the forces of the earth and used his magic to create a pedestal. He placed the icy coffin on the pedestal.

When he finished, he sensed his lovers approach. "Alexei is sleeping," Visnah whispered. "We figured you could use some help."

Ohsyn turned toward then. "I suppose it wouldn't hurt," he answered. In truth, their mere presence helped, just like it always did. However, Eva's icy sanctuary needed a few final touches. First, Visnah placed his hands over the coffin and threads of ivy emerged, shielding it in a beautiful cocoon. Zimah then took a step forward and blew over the vegetation. Instantly, it turned to solid ice. Beyond, Eva remained visible, shining like a priceless gem, but the outer shield would keep her safe. Finally, Lyetah joined them as well. He placed the sleeping Alexei down and, together, they created a circle around Eva. Their joined magic swirled around them, beautiful and intense, making Eva's sanctuary impervious to all forces. Only true love could break through now.

With the spell in place, one task remained. They needed to tell Elga and Igor of their children's fate. None of them looked forward to it.

"Let's take Alexei home," Zimah said at last. "We'll see what we can do about the rest later."

It didn't surprise Ohsyn when Zimah's reference of home turned out to be their world. Now, Alexei would no longer be able to fit in with the humans. Ohsyn wondered how Alexei would take the news when he woke. He only hoped Alexei would agree to stay with them.

Chapter 6

Alexei opened his eyes to an unfamiliar room. He blinked to clear the dizziness and focus his vision. The chamber held a surreal quality Alexei had encountered a few times before in the past days. Airy, yet hot, it was decorated in light, sunny colors, the distinctly masculine furniture complemented by the tall windows that let in cheerful rays from outside. He didn't have to think too much to realize he'd somehow ended up in his four men's home.

Memories flashed through his mind at the thought—Eva's new idea, the wolf attack, his men's appearance, and the fire consuming him whole. After one point, he only recalled shifting shadows, a blaze within him and outside him, a peculiar, unexplainable sensation of turning into something else. The pain slowly dwindled until at last, Alexei awoke on a still burning pyre with the sudden knowledge of what his lovers had been forced to do to save him. Even if he hadn't actually been awake through it, he strangely understood Lyetah had been forced to push Alexei into the fire.

And then Alexei remembered Eva's icy coffin. He couldn't help but fear for her, but in his heart, he knew all would be well. There were so many things in heaven and earth that he still didn't understand, but for whatever reason, the Goddess protected him and Eva. Alexei hoped his men would at least be able to answer some of his questions.

A warm presence materialized at his side. "You're awake," Lyetah said. "How do you feel?"

Alexei smiled at the other man. He knew the entire experience had been hardest on Lyetah. Alexei couldn't even fathom how Lyetah found the courage to do what was needed. He took his lover's hand and squeezed it. "Never better," he answered, even if some fatigue still lingered. "What about you?"

Lyetah gave him a surprised look that soon turned into bemusement. "It's so like you to worry about others when you've just barely avoided death." Lyetah's expression changed, and he seemed to close off. "Sorry about that," he finished. "I shouldn't have mentioned it."

Alexei shook his head. "It's all right. I think you suffered more than me."

And truly, he didn't have a doubt it had been so. Half the time, Alexei remained out of it while his men had been forced to acknowledge the imminence of his demise. Death was always hardest on those left behind.

Lyetah lay next to him on the bed, his warmth familiar for Alexei. As he did so, Zimah, Visnah, and Ohsyn appeared as well. With his lovers there, Alexei allowed himself to ask the questions weighing on his mind.

"Where are we?"

"This is our home," Ohsyn answered. "But I suppose we should begin at the top."

"We are earth spirits, Alexei," Visnah said. "We watch over the land wherever we are needed. In spring, we bring renewed life. In summer, heat to make the crops thrive. In autumn, bountiful harvests. In winter, we grant the earth peace to sleep and rest for the year to come. And this—where we are now—is the spirit realm. Our world."

Alexei opened his mouth and closed it back again. What did one say to such a thing? He'd expected something odd, but for some reason, it still surprised him.

It occurred to him then that he himself had done something otherworldly. He recalled summoning the weird flame that burned him so severely. What did it mean? "What about me?" he asked. "What am I?"

"You are, well, you were human," Lyetah answered hesitantly, "but both you and your sister were special.".

"Let me tell you a little story so that you'll understand better," Zimah said. "Once upon a time, there were four earth spirits. For convenience's sake, we'll call them Zimah, Visnah, Lyetah, and Ohsyn. One winter night, these spirits went out to do their job when they ran into a human couple, a man and woman we will refer to as Igor and Elga."

Alexei's mind whirled as Zimah spoke. He knew this was no story, but reality, as it had been twenty-five years back, before his birth. He and Eva had been unexpected children, appearing at an age when women rarely gave birth, a fact that many considered a miracle in the village.

Zimah spoke of the snow angel, of how through magic Alexei and Eva had been conceived. His voice became lower when he mentioned the cool heart of the ice child shadowing the warmth of the human family, and the spirits wanting to help the fire child.

"So, when chance came, the spirits approached the fire child," Zimah went on. "Only, they did not realize they would begin to feel affection for this young man." He gave Alexei an unreadable look. "I think you know what happened after that."

Alexei nodded. Now it all made sense, his vulnerability to the cold, Eva's fear of the heat, their mother's aloofness, and the voice of the fire. But he also acknowledged the undertone of Lyetah's words. He'd been a special human, but no longer. "So now what am I?"

"The Goddess tells us you are now a fire elemental," Ohsyn answered, "also a spirit, but born out of fire and with the ability to materialize in the real world."

Alexei stared at Ohsyn. He wondered if he should reply. A fire elemental? What did Alexei know about such things? He'd used the fire inside him only once, and it hadn't ended well.

Obviously guessing his misgivings, Visnah piped in, "Don't worry. It will be different than before. Last time, the flame hurt you because your mortal body couldn't contain such power. Your mortality was purged in the grove."

So that had been the purpose of the pyre. "What about Eva?"

"She remains in her sanctuary," Zimah answered. "The ice embedded with our magic prevents her spirit from slipping away. In her case, she needs someone to complete her, to fully warm her heart. A part of the chill is gone because of her connection with you, but it's not enough. She will sleep there until her fated one will find her. But, of course, we will work to help him."

"There's one more thing," Visnah added. "We still haven't notified your parents of your and Eva's situation. If you have thoughts or preferences…"

Alexei would have liked never to have to go through this, but he thanked the Goddess. She had saved them. Still, he would need his men's support. "I'd prefer it if you came with me."

Ohsyn scratched his head. "Well, actually, we'd been thinking something along the line of us going alone."

Alexei arched a brow. "You know as well as I do that doesn't make any sense. Now, help me up. They're probably worried about us by now."

Lyetah got to his feet and took Alexei in his arms. Alexei sighed. "You can put me down, you know. I'm not going to fall. I'm a… what did you say? Fire elemental, right?"

"I suppose," Lyetah murmured. He set Alexei on the floor and, together, they made their way out of the room. As his men directed him left, Alexei snuck peeks around him. He realized he must've been in Lyetah's room, since he spotted chambers that must've belonged to the other three men.

A curiosity niggled at his brain, and he couldn't help but ask, "Why do you have separate rooms?"

Visnah laughed. "Well, we weren't always lovers. In the beginning, we couldn't stand each other. Especially Zimah and Lyetah, you should have seen how they fought."

"We weren't that bad," Zimah muttered.

Visnah wrapped an arm around Alexei's waist and whispered conspiratorially, "Yes, they were."

"Now, we keep the rooms mostly for climate purposes. Like you and Eva, we have different preferences in that regard," Ohsyn explained. "But we do have a common room with a big bed. We'll show it to you later."

Alexei's face heated at the innuendo in Ohsyn's voice, and his cock hardened. He shook himself and struggled to focus on his task. Remembering where they were headed served to cool his ardor completely.

As it turned out, his men led him out of a door made out of sheer light. They emerged at the other side in the grove, between the standing stones. "This place holds a portal between the worlds," Visnah said.

Alexei bit his lip as he considered the new information. Another dilemma appeared in his mind. "How are we going to get to the house?"

Visnah chuckled. "Even earth spirits need means of transportation." He whistled and out of the blue, a green horse materialized next to Visnah. Threads of leaves and flowers entwined with its mane, and wherever it stepped, green grass sprouted. "This is a spirit horse, each of them bred for the specific purpose of taking us where we need to go."

The others followed Visnah's example, and more equines appeared, all of them modeled after their owner. Unfortunately, Alexei didn't have one, so Lyetah pulled him up on his bronze stallion.

Night engulfed them fully as they left the forest. They went so fast, that in no time, Alexei saw his parents' house ahead. As they dismounted, Zimah said, "There's something I haven't mentioned, Alexei. Your mother knows about your and Eva's origin, *lyubimiy moi*."

And the surprises went on and on.

"She does?" Alexei asked.

Zimah nodded. "It came to her in a dream, and after seeing the particularities that differentiate you from other children, she grasped the reality. But she hasn't told your father. We might have some difficulty in getting him to accept it."

As if summoned by their conversation, Alexei's father suddenly appeared on the path, riding his horse. He was no longer at an age where he could brave such weather and dangers, but the concern must have prompted him to go anyway. Thankfully, they'd come here in time.

"We'll fade from his sight until it's the right time," Zimah said. "Now go. Speak to him."

Alexei obeyed and dismounted. He waved at Igor and called out. "Papa! Over here."

Even from the distance, Alexei sensed his father's shock. Igor pushed his horse to go faster and soon reached Alexei's side.

Igor dismounted and practically pounced on Alexei, hugging him tight. "Oh, my boy, we were so worried when the horse came back without you. Are you all right?"

Alexei's eyes filled with tears at the clear evidence of his father's affection. He nodded and managed to muster an answer. "I'm fine."

Igor broke their embrace. "Where's your sister?" he asked, his eyes scanning the darkness in a desperate attempt to find Eva.

"Not here," Alexei answered. He didn't know how to say this, how to explain.

His father's expression darkened. "What do you mean? Where did you leave her?"

"Papa… I assure you there is a good reason for this." He paused and decided the best thing to do would be to take his parents to Eva. "We should go back to the house and get Mama. I have something to show you."

"Alexei, this is no time for riddles. Tell me, where is your sister?"

Alexei didn't look at his father when he replied. "I will take you to her. Please, just trust me."

"All right, son," Igor answered. He mounted the horse and gestured Alexei up. "Come, get on."

Alexei joined his father in the saddle, and they rode back the way Igor had come. Behind them, Alexei sensed his lovers following, unseen by any human eye.

It seemed to take forever for them to reach the house, but at last, they entered the courtyard, dismounted and took the animal to the stable. The door to their home burst open, and Elga rushed out. She wore thick clothing, and Alexei guessed she must have been considering leaving after them as well.

At first, she didn't spot Alexei, and she ran toward her husband. "Where are they? Where are the children?"

Alexei felt surprised she seemed concerned about him as well. "The heart of a mother is always true," Visnah said. "Her worry for you shines through the ice it's covered in now."

Alexei remembered the times when Elga's behavior would turn from cold to loving and back in mere instants. Now, he understood it. For whatever reason, the circumstances had made it so. In a sense, it brought relief to his heart, even if he'd have liked this realization to come in different circumstances.

"I'm here, Mama," he said.

Elga turned toward him. Like Igor, she rushed to hug him, but then tensed and abandoned her hold on him. "Where is Eva?" she asked, her voice cold once more.

Alexei ignored her question. He gestured them inside the stable where the temperature remained more bearable. "I think you should tell Papa about how Eva and I came to be," he finally told his mother.

Elga's eyes widened. "W–What? I don't know what you're talking about."

"Yes, you do," Alexei insisted. "Please, Mama. There's no sense in hiding it any longer."

"Alexei, what is this?" Igor asked. "Why are you disrespecting your mother? And how does this have anything to do with your sister?"

Elga remained as silent as the grave, while Zimah began to speak. "We have no choice then," he said. Together with the other three men, he emerged out of thin air. Igor jumped, turning to see who had spoken. He looked like he was going to faint, not that Alexei blamed him. "Who are you?" Igor asked them.

"We are friends," Visnah answered, "and your son speaks the truth. Come, Elga, tell him. There's nothing to be afraid of."

When faced with their appearance, Elga broke down. "It was only a dream," she whispered, "a dream and nothing more. My children are just that, children."

"Don't lie to yourself. You didn't keep Eva in a cool room for no reason," Zimah shot back. "And you, Igor. Surely you saw and wondered. How can a young girl go out in the freezing cold with nothing but a cotton dress on? Or how could Alexei stay out in the sun all day without being bothered by it?"

Igor nodded wordlessly. "If Elga is not going to say it, we will," Zimah continued. "Your children received life both from you and from two elements. You prayed for a family, and we granted you this desire through the things you most loved, snow and fire. But now, as it happens, their destiny is at a turning point."

"This is a dream," Igor said. "You are all mad."

Alexei shook his head. Taking a deep breath, he searched for the fire inside him. This time, he found it with ease. He experienced no difficulties in summoning a small blaze to his palm. It came up in the figure of Eva, a burning silhouette of her sleeping in her icy sanctuary. The reality behind the image didn't come up clear, as flame could not picture ice, but his parents grasped the essence of it.

For a few moments, he thought his father would call him a demon or something equally as horrid. But Igor did no such thing. Instead, he asked, "How did this happen? When? You were not like this when you left this morning."

"We were attacked by wolves in the forest," Alexei answered. "It just burst out. I can't explain it."

"Either way," Visnah said, "I believe you wanted to see your daughter. There are things that need to be arranged regarding her."

Igor nodded. "We will go with you. I trust Alexei. Take us to Eva."

Visnah and the others whistled once again, and the spirit horses appeared. Igor gaped and stared at the magnificent animals in dismay. "I don't suppose I can take my own, right?"

"You could, Papa," Alexei answered, "but it's so much faster on theirs." It was the understatement of the century.

Faced with this argument, Igor agreed to ride with Ohsyn. Alexei took position on Lyetah's horse again, while Elga mounted Zimah's stallion. In absolute silence, they took off toward the forest. The freezing wind intensified, but it no longer bothered Alexei so much. He didn't like it, but neither did it hurt him.

His parents, however, didn't have his luck. Even with the speed the horses ran, or perhaps because of it, the chill affected them. By the time their group reached the forest, they were visibly trembling. When Alexei dismounted, he went to his mother. She'd ridden behind Zimah, her preference for ice showing in her fascination with Zimah's white horse. Unfortunately, Zimah's nature couldn't provide any heat for her. Alexei took her hands and rubbed them between his own. As he blew into Elga's palms, he felt heat travel between him and his mother and saw her regain a healthier color. "Better?"

Elga nodded and gave him a strange look. Before Alexei could ask her about it, Visnah said, "We should go. It's best not to linger here excessively."

They entered the forest and, led by Zimah's footsteps, they headed toward the grove. Riding at full speed wasn't as an option in the woods, and Alexei's parents needed a bit of physical activity to warm them.

With a brisk and quick step, they soon reached their destination. Eva's icy sanctuary sparkled in the moonlight, drawing all gazes. Elga gasped and ran toward it. She tried to reach between the frozen vegetation to touch the ice coffin, but she couldn't.

"No one but her fated love can touch her now," Zimah said at her cry of dismay.

"Her fated love?" Igor repeated. "And how is she supposed to find this person while she's trapped and hidden here?"

"She may be trapped, but she won't be hidden," Ohsyn answered. "You will tell folk about her and ask them to come help. We will drop some words in the appropriate ears as well. It may not happen tomorrow, but her true love will come."

"How can you be so sure?" Elga sobbed, falling to her knees next her daughter's resting place. "Oh, my poor baby. How can you possibly know she will be saved?"

"The Goddess sees what we do not," Visnah answered.

Lyetah helped Elga up. "Now come. It's far too cold to stay here. She will be here tomorrow, and we will always be watching."

"You can't expect me to leave her here," Elga shot back. "Frozen, alone, in the wilderness. No. I refuse."

Her stubbornness didn't surprise Alexei. It made sense that she would not want to leave Eva. Alexei's own heart felt heavy when he acknowledged what needed to be done. But he did acknowledge it, and he realized their tears would not melt that prison of ice. They would find the person who could. "Mama, there is no other way. We must trust and hope all will be well."

Elga turned toward him, her expression torn between disbelief, relief, and pain. "I don't understand it. Why are you standing there, free of all constraint, just like before, while she is trapped beneath thick ice? I just... Oh, Alexei. I can't believe you're still alive."

She shook her head fiercely, tears streaming down her cheeks, and Alexei didn't know how to tell her the truth. It seemed to him that she'd changed. He'd expected her to blame him for surviving when Eva hadn't. Instead, she seemed torn between doing so, and being thankful he'd lived. He decided to hide the glum details from her. "Mama, I'm not like before," he whispered. "I can't go back either."

Elga froze. She obviously hadn't expected his words. "W-What do you mean?"

Strikingly, Igor spoke next, revealing what Alexei wanted to hide. "You were trapped, too, but in fire." Alexei's father stared somewhere to their right, and when Alexei looked that way, he realized Igor spotted the remnants of the pyre.

"I don't understand," Elga said. She followed Igor's gaze to the pyre. "This is some sort of weird nightmare."

Alexei wanted to comfort them, to tell them the pyre had been there for ceremonial purposes alone. But the lie wouldn't leave his lips. Thankfully, Zimah intervened. "The important thing is that both Alexei and Eva are safe. Since he cannot live with you any longer, he will come with us."

"Where?" Igor asked. "Where will you go?"

Alexei nearly broke down right then and there at the sorrow in his father's voice. "Papa, I will always be with you. I promise. And I will be watching over Eva. You needn't fear a thing."

He didn't know if they believed him or not, but after much insistence, his parents in the end agreed to return home. During the trip back home, everything still felt very surreal. After they said their good-byes, his shaken parents entered the house, leaving him standing outside with his men. For a few moments, the situation didn't really compute. He'd no longer live here. He'd lost his life and his home.

It was a strange thing that he'd never panicked about this until now. But he'd been concerned about Eva, and now that he'd made certain she'd be safe, the rest struck him with full force. Visnah wrapped his arms around him and whispered, "It's all right, Alexei. You'll always have a home with us."

He mounted with Alexei on his stallion and together, they once more headed the way they'd come. Alexei didn't register much of the ride, and before he knew it, they'd reached his men's house in the spirit world.

Visnah led him to a large room which held the huge bed. Alexei identified it as "the common room" mentioned before. "You can get some sleep here," Visnah said as he placed Alexei down on the soft sheets.

Ohsyn smiled at him. "You definitely need it. Don't worry. We'll watch over you."

Lyetah and Zimah didn't speak, but their mere presence served as testament to their agreement.

"Come lay down by me," Alexei said. He guessed that if the bed fit four large men, it would fit five.

His lovers obeyed and joined him on the comfortable sheets. Alexei ended up spooned between Lyetah and Zimah. He closed his eyes and forced himself to relax. At one point, he must've dozed off, but he awoke when he felt something amiss.

As the sleepiness faded, he realized he now slept in an empty bed. Startled, he looked around, only to spot his men sitting on various chairs and settees around the room. "What are you doing?"

Lyetah gave him a strained smile. "We couldn't sleep and we didn't want to bother you."

Alexei arched a brow. "It's your absence that bothers me."

Oddly, none of them replied. As he took in their stance, however, Alexei understood. Judging about the single sexual experience they'd shared, they were clearly attracted to him. Proximity would make their attraction rise to the fore.

Heat awoke inside Alexei as his body responded to the mere recollection of one their time together. He wanted it again. He wanted it so badly, but it seemed his men intended to do the noble thing and allow him to rest.

Perhaps he should have followed their lead and simply gone back to sleep, but neither his body nor his heart allowed him to do so. "Please," he whispered. "Make me feel like I'm home like you said."

Lyetah got up from his seat and knelt next to the bed. He gripped Alexei's hand and squeezed it. "Oh, Alexei. You don't have to do this."

Alexei used Lyetah's hold on his hand to pull the other man on the bed. Taken by surprise, Lyetah fell face front on the soft mattress. Alexei flipped him over and promptly pounced, attacking Lyetah's mouth. At first, Lyetah seemed too shocked to respond, but soon, passion and instinct took over, and the other man began his own assault on Alexei's senses. His hands caressed Alexei's back and went down to knead his buttocks.

When the kiss broke, Alexei lifted his head and stared down at Lyetah. "Stop thinking I'm some fragile flower. I know what I want."

The answer came from Zimah. "So it would seem."

Alexei looked toward Zimah and saw him, Visnah, and Ohsyn approach. They joined Alexei and Lyetah on the huge bed, and Alexei's daring melted as he realized exactly what he'd initiated. But he could not back down now. He refused to.

His men must have guessed his thoughts. Their clothing dissipated into thin air. Alexei licked his lips as all that naked skin became revealed in front of his greedy eyes. He wondered if he could pull off this little trick, too, because he certainly couldn't muster enough coherence to disrobe the traditional way. He tried to will it to happen and a tingle over his skin signaled his own clothes vanish. He didn't realize he'd achieved his goal until he felt Lyetah's warm hand on his skin.

"You're so beautiful, *solnyshko moyo*," Lyetah murmured.

Visnah crawled toward them, drawing Alexei's attention to him. "You two look so amazing together." He pressed his lips to Alexei's in a gentle, yet insistent kiss. It felt almost as if the hidden passion within Visnah's tender nature started to become unleashed. Their tongues dueled in a lazy, delicious dance that promised so much more.

When they broke apart, Visnah pressed Alexei down to lay on top of Lyetah. Alexei ended up chest to chest with Lyetah, his naked ass up and exposed to the other three men. He felt Lyetah's erection against his own hard cock and couldn't help but rub against his lover. Lyetah crushed their lips together once more, and as they kissed, Alexei felt a slick finger prod at his backside.

At the surprising sensation, Alexei tensed a bit. He'd done some exploring in that area, but no one else had touched him there so far. But Lyetah's mouth felt so good on his own that he didn't have any trouble in relaxing and accepting the touch. Even without seeing, he knew who it belonged to. Ohsyn's contained strength always swept over him decadently, like sweet flowing wine, just like now.

Ohsyn pressed his finger deep inside Alexei, pushing it in and out of Alexei's passage. Sparks flew over his skin as Ohsyn hit a certain spot inside Alexei. Any discomfort or misgiving vanished, Alexei's body demanding to be taken. Ohsyn stretched him gently, preparing him for further invasion, but the caresses soon began to be insufficient. Alexei thrust against Ohsyn's digit, then back against Lyetah's cock. Kissing, being touched so intimately, it all felt so amazing, but Alexei wanted more, so much more.

All of a sudden, Lyetah disappeared from beneath him and reappeared to his right. Before Alexei could figure out how his lover had done that, Lyetah gestured him on all fours. The shift separated him from Ohsyn, but Alexei ended up with Lyetah's cock pointing at him. The hard shaft looked delicious and Alexei wanted nothing else but to have it deep in his mouth. "Come on, *miliy moi*," Ohsyn whispered. "Suck him."

Alexei obediently parted his lips and Lyetah pushed his dick inside. A myriad of flavors exploded on Alexei's tongue, Lyetah's taste even stronger now. He wiggled his ass, wordlessly begging for more. Ohsyn thrust two fingers into his wanton hole, and Alexei moaned. Above him, Lyetah groaned and began to thrust inside Alexei's mouth.

At first, it was difficult to get used to such a large thing invading his mouth. To a certain extent, it distracted Alexei, and he gagged, unable to take his lover fully. A distant thought made him realize he was in the spirit world. Anything would be possible, if he just focused and tried. He breathed through his nose and focused on relaxing. With each passing second, it became easier and easier, until he could actually take his lover fully. With each motion from Lyetah's hips, Alexei's arousal increased more and more. He could almost bury his face in his lover's pubes now, and the scent drove him wild. Even so, he focused on giving his lover pleasure. He must have been doing something right because Lyetah's grunts of passion increased in volume.

Ohsyn's fingers retreated, and Alexei felt something harder and much larger prod at his backside. This was it, the moment he'd been waiting for. Lyetah stilled, gently caressing Alexei's hair, soothing him. And then, Ohsyn pushed inside, stretching him, hurting him so deliciously. Alexei's eyes filled with tears, half of pain, half of awe. But Ohsyn went slow, so slow and careful. By the time Alexei felt Ohsyn's balls flush against his ass, he'd already begun to get accustomed to the sensation of being filled.

Like Lyetah, Ohsyn was generously endowed, and being pierced from two directions overwhelmed Alexei. For a few seconds, he feared to even breathe, lest he break the amazing spell. It just didn't seem possible that he'd be able to take their mammoth cocks inside him.

A male groan from his side drew his attention. With the corner of his eye, Alexei caught sight of Zimah and Visnah together, naked, touching each other's hard cocks. "You look so beautiful, *radost moia*, so very beautiful," Visnah said.

Their eyes on him fascinated him. It felt as if their gazes turned into a palpable touch. When Zimah tweaked Visnah's nipple, Alexei felt it as well. Their hands seemed to engulf his own hard shaft, jacking him in slow, sensual pumps.

Alexei whimpered as sensations swamped him. Ohsyn and Lyetah pulled out of him at the same time, then thrust back in. Lyetah pushed in and out of his mouth, the incredible heat of his dick finding an echo in Alexei's flame. Ohsyn's cock filled him over and over, his motions deep, hard, and steady, his rhythm slow and penetrating. When Ohsyn hit that special spot inside, sparks of energy flowed over Alexei. He could feel his orgasm approach, so close, just within his reach.

Zimah and Visnah's eyes continued to watch him, as if fucking him just through their eyes. Alexei became a receptacle of his lovers' pleasure, With each thrust from Ohsyn and Lyetah, he drowned more and more in the sensation. His anus throbbed, stretched by Ohsyn's cock, and his jaw hurt from Lyetah's enthusiastic thrusts. But such limits meant nothing, not anymore, not in this world and with the lovers bringing him so much pleasure. Alexei let everything go, losing his fears, until the slight pain dwindled into a beautiful burn, like the sun dancing over his skin.

Under the assault of his lovers, Alexei couldn't resist for much longer. Being taken and branded like this went beyond every dream he'd ever had. Sandwiched between the passion of two men, spoiled by the attention of two others, he found his peak. His orgasm took him in an overflow of sensation so intense Alexei almost thought he could not survive it. He'd never thought he could experience more pleasure than he had in the grove, but this amazing union nearly drove him crazy.

Just when he thought it couldn't get any better, Lyetah and Ohsyn came, too, filling his ass and mouth with their seed. It made everything so much better, and his climax went on and on, fueled by Lyetah's heat and Ohsyn's intoxicating scent. In one perfect instant, Alexei felt his fire element blend with Lyetah's blazing passion and Ohsyn's decadent and wicked generosity. For a few moments, he must've blacked out because when he recovered, Ohsyn and Lyetah had moved away, with Zimah and Visnah taking their respective positions.

In the aftermath of his amazing orgasm, Alexei's body turned pliant and relaxed. Zimah thrust his own hard shaft inside Alexei's ass. Alexei's hole greedily took in the new invasion, while Visnah's dick invaded Alexei's mouth.

Unlike Ohsyn, Zimah chose an almost punishing rhythm, fucking him hard. In and out, violent and raw, he simply let go. His chill reached out to the flame inside Alexei, but instead of clashing, they molded together in the perfect balance. Their dance went on with the soft breeze of Visnah's heart joining them within Alexei. As always, Visnah went slow, drawing the sensations out, allowing Alexei to savor the act, pushing farther every time, until at last, Alexei took him into his throat. Having them so deeply within him arose renewed pleasure inside Alexei. His cock hardened once again, throbbing, demanding release.

As if intending to short-circuit Alexei's brain, Lyetah and Ohsyn lay down next to him. Lyetah slid under him and began laving his balls, engulfing them in wet heat. Occasionally, the naughty touch reached Alexei's perineum, caressing him in a delicious torture. Ohsyn's hands traveled over his back and chest, awakening every possible nerve.

In no time, Alexei reached the brink of orgasm again. This time, it took him by complete surprise, washing away his very sanity, every barrier he might have considered having.

His mind could no longer take the amazing pleasure, and he lost track of all else except his lovers. When Zimah and Visnah found their peaks, too, Alexei surrendered the battle and slid into unconsciousness.

He awoke exhausted but content in the huge bed. This time, however, his lovers remained by his side. Cuddled between Lyetah and Zimah, Alexei closed his eyes and fell asleep.

Chapter 7

Two years later

Alexei plopped down on the ground next to the standing stones, disappointment coursing through him. Yet another day had gone by with no luck for his sister.

Like they'd promised, his lovers sent word through the realm of Eva's distress. Aided by his parents, Alexei led people to the grove, one by one. He'd seen so many men come to try to free his sister. Even women showed up, much to his parents' distress. From powerful warlords to peasants, none of them managed to break the icy barrier. Alexei's lovers had told him that one day, her true love would arrive to rescue her, but Alexei now wondered when it would happen, if it ever did.

"Don't despair, *lyubimiy moi*," Zimah said as he sat down next to Alexei. "Her time will come. You just have to be patient."

Alexei sighed and leaned against Zimah. He felt thankful that at least one of his lovers always made it his business to stay with Alexei when he watched over his sister, even if they had important jobs as earth spirits. Their presence helped him deal with the never-ending frustration.

"I suppose that's it for today," Alexei said as he stole a look toward the darkening sky. People had been warned to stay away from the forest at night. Wolves still presented a problem for mortals, even if they couldn't hurt Alexei anymore.

"Do you want to go home?" Zimah asked. "The others will return soon as well."

Alexei nodded and got up. His parents had left a little while ago, so any new arrivals would have to wait until tomorrow.

Just as they headed toward the standing stones, Zimah stopped. "There's another presence approaching," he said.

Surprise gripped Alexei. Who could have come here at this hour, risking an attack from wild animals? They waited next to Eva's sanctuary until at last, a knight and his squire emerged in the grove. Alexei analyzed the new arrival with a critical eye. He seemed like the proverbial standard for a knight in shining armor. In fact, the armor gleamed even in the dim light. The man looked powerful and foreign, and Alexei felt a small stirring of hope. Could this be Eva's fated love? "Here she is," the knight whispered more to himself than to anyone else.

He approached Eva's coffin with the squire pulling a white stallion along. At last, he reached the icy sanctuary and placed his hand on the frozen vegetation. Behind him, the squire took in the sight with wide eyes.

Nothing happened. The knight retrieved his long broadsword and hit the outer shield of ice with it. The weapon recoiled with such force it went flying out of the man's hand. The knight himself staggered and caught himself on his squire.

After a few seconds, he managed to gather his wits and went to retrieve his sword. "Oh, well," he said. "I guess it was a useless journey after all."

"But, My Lord, we can't just leave her," the squire protested.

The knight shrugged. "There are many other damsels in distress where this one came from. I'll just save another to make her my queen. Come on, Vadik. We must get some rest before we leave this damn village tomorrow."

The squire—Vadik—turned to look one more time toward Eva, before nodding. "Yes, My Lord." Together, the two of them disappeared into the night.

After he watched them go, Alexei turned toward his lover. "What did you think?"

Zimah smiled at him, his blue eyes shining in the darkness. "I think Eva found her true love."

* * * *

The night signaled a change in Alexei's routine. The knight never did return, but the next day, the squire, Vadik, came with Igor and Elga.

Nothing happened when he touched the ice either. He didn't look surprised, but smiled sadly at Alexei's parents.

"Well, I didn't really expect someone like her would be fated for someone like me." He paused, then caressed the ice almost absently. "I know this is presumptuous," he told them, "but I'd like to stay and help you. She... Yesterday, I just... I can't explain it, but even if I can't be with her, I don't want to leave either. I heard you lost your son as well, so if you'd have me, I'd love to help you in whatever way I can."

Igor looked shocked. "But, my boy, you can have a brilliant future ahead of you. You can't just throw all that away to live in a forgotten village."

Vadik smiled. "It's just the way I feel."

"Then our house is open to you," Elga said. "My son is still watching over us and Eva, but you can be our second one."

Truth be told, Alexei did indeed come to help his parents from time to time, unseen and unheard by anyone from the outside. The villagers had begun to push his parents away after Eva's entrapment and his disappearance. They believed Igor and Elga to be cursed. It impressed Alexei that this man would agree to stay here and face their problems, just because he didn't want to abandon Eva.

As it turned out, Zimah's prediction proved to be correct. As the days and weeks passed, Vadik continued to visit Alexei's sister. The ice never cracked when he touched it, but Alexei did notice it begin to melt. At times, he almost heard Eva speak, and he swore Vadik could hear her as well.

His guess was confirmed when, at last, one beautiful autumn day, the shield around Eva shattered and her icy coffin melted. Vadik helped her out of her former sanctuary. They threw their arms around each other, with Vadik whispering endearments in her ear and Eva desperately clinging to him.

"Thank you for waiting for me," she said.

"How could I not, my darling? How could I not?"

They didn't see Alexei and his lovers standing there, and when they sat on the grass, Alexei chose not to bother them. However, just as he readied himself to go, a stifled sob from Eva drew his attention. "I wish Alexei could be here, too," she said. "He'd be so happy for me."

Alexei gaped, for the first time understanding she thought him to be dead. Vadik hugged her tight, obviously not knowing how to comfort her and very distressed about it.

Alexei needed no other sign to make his appearance. "I am happy for you," he said as he allowed his mortal form to manifest. His lovers had explained Eva's spirit had never passed through the same transformation as him, so she would not be able to see them unless he willed it.

In a flash, Eva turned to face him. Her blue eyes turned almost aquamarine with volatile emotion. Physically, she hadn't changed at all, and yet, she looked nothing like the sister who'd sent him trekking through the freezing cold to gather violets.

After one moment during which she just stared at him, she shot to her feet and rushed to him. Her slender arms hugged his torso so tight Alexei wouldn't have thought it possible, not from her. "Alexei, you're alive. I can't believe it. But Vadik... Vadik said..."

"It's a long and complicated story," Alexei told his sister. "I am alive, just not like you and Mama." For all purposes, he had indeed died, but he'd managed to pass to a different level of existence. Eva would remain a human, as she'd never gone beyond into the spirit world. But Alexei no longer feared for her, not now, that she'd found her true level.

Eva opened her mouth and closed it. "You're a ghost?" she murmured, her lower lip trembling as if she tried to keep herself from crying.

Alexei chuckled and ruffled her hair. "Do I look like a ghost?"

As children, it always irritated Eva to have her hair messy, but now it didn't seem to bother her. Instead, she hugged him again. "As long as you're by my side and you're happy, you can be anything you like."

"I'm happy," Alexei answered. "So very happy."

His men chose this moment to materialize. Their appearance served to snap Vadik out of his shock. He hastened to Eva's side, sword drawn.

"It's all right," Alexei immediately said. "They're with me." He didn't know how to explain all four of them were his lovers.

Eva frowned at Zimah, and after a few tense seconds, she cried out, "I remember you," she said. "You're the one who stuck me inside that awful thing." She pointed at Lyetah. "And you threw Alexei into the fire." Her entire stance tense and angry, she glared at Alexei. "What are you doing with them, Alexei?"

"Eva, they saved us. We were attacked by wolves." Taking a deep breath, he took the plunge and decided to tell her everything. "You and I had a power deep inside. You felt it that day, didn't you, the freezing cold?"

Eva nodded. "How did you know about that?"

"Well, I had fire. We were granted this power from birth, but during the wolf attack, it burst out too violently and threatened to consume us. What they did needed to be done to keep us from dying."

Eva seemed to contemplate his words. She closed her eyes, and Alexei knew she now tested her own body and soul to see if she could still feel the chill. "You're right," she said at last. "I don't understand it, but you're right."

"We'll explain everything in time," Zimah piped in. "Don't worry, your power is nothing to be afraid of as long as you know how to use it."

Vadik gaped at him. "Power? Magic? This... This is all so odd."

Eva turned to her rescuer. "Does it change anything?" she asked sadly.

Vadik took her hands and kissed them. "No! Of course not. I'll get used to it. It's just a lot to take in."

Alexei didn't blame the man. Now, he didn't know whether to finish the tale and reveal his relationship with his men. He wasn't ashamed of it, but Vadik might not understand.

Eva must have sense his distress and gave him a sidelong glance. "What is it, Alexei? There's something else, isn't there? Who are they really?"

Now that she'd asked, Alexei had no choice but to tell her. Pointing at each of his men, he introduced them. "This is Visnah, Lyetah, Ohsyn, and Zimah. They are my lovers."

Vadik looked like he was about to faint, and Eva looked from him to his men, as if analyzing them. "Are you serious, Alexei? Men? And four of them?"

Alexei nodded, to which Eva said, "Wow. How does that work? Never mind, don't tell me. I don't want to know." She smiled at him. "As long as you're happy and safe, I can accept it."

"You don't look all that surprised," Alexei answered, confused.

"Well, I'm certainly surprised about the number, but I already suspected you liked other men. And I'm guessing you're the ones who gave Alexei the violets, berries, and apples."

"Indeed, we are," Zimah answered. "I trust you won't make such unreasonable requests in the future."

Eva's expression turned shamed, and Visnah gave Zimah a chastising look. "Let's not think about that now," he said. "Today is a day of celebration. Let your parents know as they've been very worried about you."

"There's nothing quite like being young and in love," Lyetah continued. "Enjoy it!"

"And don't worry, we'll take care of Alexei," Ohsyn finished.

"Thank you," Eva said. "I... I promise I'll be a better person from now on. Thank you."

Alexei hugged his sister silently telling her he didn't keep any grudges for the past. How could he? She was his twin, and he loved her. He looked at Vadik and gave the man his best threatening look. "You be good to her."

He must've put a bit of fire in his eyes as Vadik looked taken aback. Thankfully, the man recovered and nodded. "I will."

They said their good-byes, and Alexei watched Vadik lead Eva away toward the main road. "That went well," Visnah said.

Tremendous relief swamped Alexei at his lover's words. All through these years, he'd felt guilty over living his amazing love story, while Eva remained trapped under thick ice. But no longer. Now, they could both be happy, with their true loves, a fairy tale come true for both of them.

"It did, indeed," he answered. "Let's go home."

Epilogue

"I now pronounce you man and wife. You may kiss the bride."

Upon the priest's words, Eva and Vadik kissed, sealing their union. Pride and happiness swelled inside Alexei at the sight. She looked so beautiful in her traditional wedding garb, and Vadik clearly worshipped the ground she walked on. They might not be royalty, but they certainly looked more beautiful than any prince and princess in the world. Now, the two had bonded their destinies until death do them apart.

His parents had prepared quite a lavish feast afterwards, and many of those who'd attempted to rescue Eva had come. Alexei's lovers helped, providing a lot of the fruit and vegetables needed. It was quite a shock for everyone who'd ever spoken ill of them, but Igor and Elga explained that with their daughter's freedom came the blessing of the Goddess. Alexei couldn't have put it better himself.

He did wish he could have joined in on the rest of celebration, but in the end, it didn't matter, not when Eva threw a gaze in his direction and smiled. Only she, Vadik, and their parents could see him and his lovers standing there right next to the priest. It was enough.

The priest spoke some more of the importance of the step they'd taken and the sanctity of their union. When at last the ceremony ended, Alexei felt a bit saddened. He watched his family party and rejoice but could not go to them. But then, Visnah wrapped his arm around Alexei's waist, and just like that, Alexei's melancholy began to fade. He had a new family now, and so did Eva.

He waved at his sister. She discreetly broke away from the guests and made her way toward him. "Are you leaving already?" she asked.

Alexei chuckled. "There's no point in staying if I can't get drunk." Leaving all jokes aside, he added, "Be happy, Eva. You deserve it."

Eva hugged him tightly. "Thank you for everything. I'll see you soon, all right?"

Alexei nodded. Eva and Vadik had decided to stay here and build a quiet life, just like Igor and Elga. It would not be the last time they saw each other.

After saying good night to his parents, they headed out. The horses took them back to the forest with accustomed speed, and soon they reached the grove. They went through the portal beyond the standing stones and at last reached the spirit world.

"Home at last," Lyetah said. His hands went around Alexei's waist and he nibbled on Alexei's ear. "Weddings always make me horny," he whispered.

Alexei broke away from Lyetah and threw a spark of fire at him. "Don't be crass. It's my sister we're talking about."

"Well, your sister is happy with her new husband. Perhaps we should get happy, too?"

Lyetah wiggled his eyebrows. Secretly, Alexei wanted what his lover offered. But truth be told, Alexei felt a bit jealous of Eva. He'd have liked a marriage ceremony as well to bind them together.

"What is it, Alexei?" Lyetah asked, now sounding serious. "You've grown silent all of a sudden."

Alexei realized they were all giving him concerned looks, and he offered them a smile. "I suppose I wanted something like that for myself."

Visnah blinked in confusion while Zimah visibly tensed. "A wife?" he asked.

Alexei almost burst into laughter. "No! A wedding."

"Oh, *miliy moi*," Ohsyn said. He hugged Alexei and kissed his forehead. "We don't need a wedding. Don't you know? We already have our destinies united."

Alexei knew that, of course, but in his heart, he sensed the need to mark it somehow. As if guessing his thoughts, Visnah clapped his hands together and said, "Perhaps we should hold one, too, just for us, here."

In the blink of an eye, Alexei found himself in the garden, his lovers by his side. Out of nowhere, beautiful adornments materialized, delicate snowflakes somehow managing to coexist with the sunny rays coming from above. Flowers bloomed everywhere, filling the garden with their intoxicating perfume. Heavy fruit hung from the trees, begging to be plucked out and bitten into. It was simply perfect, everything his lovers meant and represented molded into one.

In the center of the garden lay the altar where they all said their prayers to the Goddess. "Come," Ohsyn said.

Lost in awe, Alexei knelt in front of the altar with his lovers. Hand in hand, they bowed their heads. Visnah spoke first. "I love these men with all my heart. Please, Goddess, bless our union."

Each of his men prayed to the Goddess for the same thing, until at last, Alexei's turn came. "I do not know what I've done to deserve this gift, but I am forever thankful for it. Please, Goddess, bless our union."

A cone of white light seemed to engulf them, and Alexei felt the power flow over him. Through it, he actually saw in his men's minds, experienced their emotions, their love for each other and for him. He didn't know how long they just knelt there, but when at last the light faded, Alexei knew he'd been given the blessing he'd yearned for.

For a little while, they remained in the garden, thanking the Goddess for their gift. Then they got up, and birds appeared around them, singing a cheerful symphony.

They danced, and laughed, and ate sweet-tasting fruit. Alexei felt happier than he'd ever been. Perhaps he couldn't party with the villagers, but a private celebration with just him and his men ended up so much better.

The garden faded around them, and they emerged into their bedroom. None wasted any time with clothing. Alexei couldn't have been more grateful for it. He had no idea how this day ended up his wedding day as well as Eva's, but it meant so much to him. The emotion fueled his desire for his men, and he ached to bring their bodies together.

They fell together onto the bed, five pairs of hands roaming fiercely on every inch of naked skin they could reach. Alexei ended up sandwiched between Zimah and Lyetah with Ohsyn behind Lyetah and Visnah next to Zimah. Lyetah's slick finger penetrated his passage while Zimah's tongue invaded his mouth. As Lyetah mercilessly rubbed his prostate, Alexei moaned at the dual assault, his body hot and needing more.

Zimah's mouth abandoned his far too soon, and at the same time, Lyetah's fingers left his body. Alexei felt bereft, left without an anchor, but he didn't get the chance to protest. Lyetah's cock nudged at his hole and, in one single, almost brutal thrust, his lover impaled him. The delicious burn spread all throughout him, awakening the blaze inside his heart.

But Lyetah didn't move, instead waiting fully within Alexei, filling him to the brink. Alexei desperately wanted friction. "Please," he croaked out. "Fuck me."

He understood Lyetah's actions when another deep thrust came from behind. Lyetah groaned as Ohsyn penetrated him, the shove sending him ever deep inside Alexei. Alexei cried out, the strength behind the impalement nearly sending him flying forward.

Zimah caught him before that could happen. He caressed the side of Alexei's face, and Alexei shuddered as the cool touch tingled over his skin. "So beautiful, *lyubimiy moi*," Zimah whispered almost reverently.

Zimah's hard cock was just inches away from Alexei's mouth. Alexei somehow managed to muster enough coherence to reach out and direct it to his mouth. Ohsyn's hold on his hip kept him steady as he did so, and Zimah groaned when Alexei fully took his dick into his mouth.

Zimah tasted amazing, the flavor of his pre-cum both familiar and exciting. The chill always coming from Zimah called out to the blaze within Alexei, summoning it to the surface. Greed and lust rose within Alexei, and he devoured his lover's prick, finding pleasure in each delicious inch that entered his mouth.

The two men behind him began a steady rhythm, each motion from Ohsyn echoing into Alexei twofold through Lyetah. Mirroring their movements, Zimah fucked Alexei's mouth steadily. Alexei lost himself in the sensation, and his only niggling desire was to feel Visnah as well.

As if sensing his thoughts, Visnah approached Zimah from behind. Alexei's arousal pulsed even brighter as he watched Visnah work his fingers inside Zimah. He couldn't quite see the real action from his position, but he could very well guess by Zimah's increasing unsteadiness and what he spotted of Visnah's touches on their wintry lover.

They all slowed down, allowing Visnah to prepare Zimah at leisure. Already, Alexei could feel Visnah's touches deep within him. His own pleasure increased when Visnah hit Zimah's prostate, massaging the gland with expert motions. Urgency filled Alexei, and he'd have begged his lovers to hurry if he didn't have his mouth full of cock. Still, his men seemed to feel the same need. The ghostly fingers disappeared, and finally, Visnah slid in, and it felt like a surreal connection clicked into place. The angle of penetration became somewhat awkward, but all of a sudden, Alexei found himself floating in the air, his men moving up against him, and never once getting dislodged from his body. Reality—even the relative one in the spiritual world—melted around him, and Alexei felt all his men inside him, so deep, possessing him so utterly it humbled him.

The thrusts began gentle, like his men's first touches had been. The memory of sweet kisses stolen in a grove flashed through

Alexei's mind. Gradually, the pace increased, and Lyetah's dick hit Alexei's special spot, sending violent flames of ecstasy through him. Through his mind's eye, he saw himself in the very same grove, experiencing his first climax at the hands of another. Zimah also began to move faster, Visnah's thrusts inside him urging him on until Zimah's dick hit the back of Alexei's throat. Perhaps if he'd been mortal, Alexei would have choked or gagged. He'd actually done so once, during their first time together. But Alexei had a two-year experience in surpassing the remnants of his human life, and he had no trouble taking Zimah fully. Even as he tasted Zimah's abundant precum on his tongue, he remembered the day when they'd first made love in this very same room.

On and on, it went, memories blending with the present, love mixing with lust. An unbearable ache spread through Alexei. Feeling his lovers so close, bonded to each other, drove him wild, and he wanted this moment to last forever. And yet, he desperately needed to come. Pleasure radiated from his ass with each of Lyetah and Ohsyn's thrusts. Every time Ohsyn pushed inside Lyetah, Alexei's oversensitized body experienced the ecstasy in a double dose. Similarly, with each of Visnah's motions, Zimah grew wilder and wilder, taking what he wanted, fucking Alexei's mouth with abandon and making the fire within Alexei reach out to them all.

The pace increased beyond anything humanly possible. The world became a blur, the symphony of their moving bodies echoing deep within them. Alexei felt every thrust into his very soul. Ohsyn's cock massaged Alexei's hole from within, the delicious friction increasing with the echoing sensations coming from Zimah.

As much as he wanted the make this last, the intensity of the experience didn't allow it. The realization and full acknowledgement that he belonged to these men forever gave him the complete happiness he'd ached for during these past years, the freedom to love and be loved with no restraint and no regret. United in body and soul with his lovers, Alexei exploded, the climax consuming his very being almost greedily, wiping away anything that didn't belong to him or his lovers.

One last thrust, and Lyetah filled Alexei with hot seed. It scorched Alexei inside out, and his power broke loose, making bright flames burst into the room. And yet, Zimah didn't seem affected. If anything, he shone even brighter in the light of the burning. With a groan, Zimah buried himself deep inside Alexei's mouth and sent his essence down Alexei's throat.

Physically, Alexei didn't feel Ohsyn and Visnah peak, but he didn't need to. In the end, they weren't beings of the flesh, but they belonged to the spirit world. Their pleasure flared through him as clearly as Lyetah and Zimah's had.

Ecstasy swallowed Alexei whole, his climax prolonged to infinity by those of his lovers. No, his husbands. They were his husbands now. Perhaps they'd been so from the very moment he'd come to live here, but Alexei's mind had not been able to understand the concept. He understood it now, and the emotions that swamped him went beyond all imagination.

When he at last began to recover, the sexual satisfaction turned into bliss. But his relaxation didn't last as the spell that held them aloft ended. Alexei yelped as he fell onto the bed.

Chuckles sounded from above him and Alexei looked up at his still floating men. "You think this is funny?" he growled at them. "That's it. Starting this moment, you're not getting any."

Zimah grinned. "You don't say, *lyubimiy moi?*" He shared a look with the others, and Alexei felt the wicked intent behind it. "That sounds like a challenge to me."

They descended upon him again, and as they took him over and over, Alexei prayed for it to last forever. At some point, he'd lost his heart to the four seasons, and he never wanted to get it back.

THE END

HTTP://SCARLETHYACINTH.WEBS.COM

ABOUT THE AUTHOR

A native Romanian, Scarlet was born in 1986 and grew up an avid fan of Karl May and Jules Verne, reading fantasy stories and adventure. Later, when she was out of fantasy stories to read, she delved into her mother's collection of books and, of course, stumbled onto romance.

As a writer though, Scarlet Hyacinth was born one sunny summer day, when a dear friend of hers—the same friend who introduced her to GLBT fiction—proposed they start writing a story of their own. As it turns out, the two friends never did finish that particular story, but Scarlet discovered she had a knack for writing and ended up starting to write individually. And so, between working on her dissertation, studying for exams, and reading yaoi manga, she started writing the Kaldor Saga. Along the way, Scarlet met a lot of wonderful people who supported her, and in the end, she found her story a home and, in the process, fulfilled a beautiful dream.

Also by Scarlet Hyacinth

Siren Classic ManLove: Kaldor Saga 1: *Enraptured*
Siren Classic ManLove: Kaldor Saga 2: *Over the Edge*
Siren Classic ManLove: Kaldor Saga 3: *Destinies in Darkness, Part 1*
Siren Classic ManLove: Kaldor Saga 3: *Destinies in Darkness, Part 2*
Siren Classic ManLove: Kaldor Saga 4: *Mending Shattered Souls*
Siren Allure ManLove: *Truth and Deception*
Siren Classic ManLove: Sequel to *Truth and Deception*: *Reborn*
Siren Classic ManLove: Deadly Mates 1: *Moon's Sweet Poison*
Siren Classic ManLove: Deadly Mates 2: *Wings of Moonlight*
Ménage Amour ManLove: Deadly Mates 3: *Spell of the Predator's Moon*
Ménage Amour ManLove: Deadly Mates 4: *Dragon's Bloodmoon*
Ménage Amour ManLove: Spirit Wolves 1: *A Mate Beyond Their Reach*
Ménage Amour ManLove: Spirit Wolves 2: *Mates in Life and Death*
Ménage Amour ManLove: Spirit Wolves 3: *Two Mates for a Magistrate*
Ménage Amour ManLove: Spirit Wolves 4: *Three Mates, One Destiny*
Ménage Amour ManLove: Spirit Wolves 5: *Star-Crossed Mates*

Available at
BOOKSTRAND.COM

Siren Publishing, Inc.
www.SirenPublishing.com

CPSIA information can be obtained at www.ICGtesting.com
Printed in the USA
LVOW082202060512

280597LV00006B/80/P